Shane Night Wind Intrigued Her.

Even his name stirred an engaging image—this man who rescued cougars, picked wildflowers in the rain, braided his hair. This Comanche warrior who had burned sage in a purifying ceremony to grant serenity to her unborn child.

"Thank you," Kelly said. "For thinking of the baby."

"You're welcome."

She wanted to take his hand and place it against her tummy. The baby was moving gently—a tiny angel fluttering its wings, cleansed and whole, awaiting the world.

She couldn't stop herself from saying, "I've never met anyone like you before."

Shane's lips tilted into a small smile. "Nor I you."

Dear Reader,

Our 20th anniversary pledge to you, our devoted readers, is a promise to continue delivering passionate, powerful, provocative love stories from your favorite Silhouette Desire authors for all the years to come!

As an anniversary treat, we've got a special book for you from the incomparable Annette Broadrick. *Marriage Prey* is a romance between the offspring of two couples from Annette's earliest Desire books, which Silhouette reissued along with a third early Desire novel last month as *Maximum Marriage: Men on a Mission.* Bestselling author Mary Lynn Baxter brings you November's MAN OF THE MONTH...*Her Perfect Man.* A minister and a reformed party girl fall for each other in this classic opposites-attract love story. *A Cowboy's Gift* is the latest offering by RITA Award winner Anne McAllister in her popular CODE OF THE WEST miniseries.

Another RITA winner, Caroline Cross, delivers the next installment of the exciting Desire miniseries FORTUNE'S CHILDREN: THE GROOMS with *Husband—or Enemy?* Dixie Browning's miniseries THE PASSIONATE POWERS continues with *The Virgin and the Vengeful Groom,* part of our extra-sensual BODY & SOUL promotion. And Sheri WhiteFeather has created another appealing Native American hero in *Night Wind's Woman.*

So please join us in celebrating twenty glorious years of category romance by indulging yourself with all six of these compelling love stories from Silhouette Desire!

Enjoy!

Joan Marlow Golan

Joan Marlow Golan
Senior Editor, Silhouette Desire

Please address questions and book requests to:
Silhouette Reader Service
U.S.: 3010 Walden Ave., P.O. Box 1325, Buffalo, NY 14269
Canadian: P.O. Box 609, Fort Erie, Ont. L2A 5X3

Night Wind's Woman
SHERI WHITEFEATHER

Silhouette®

Desire®

Published by Silhouette Books

America's Publisher of Contemporary Romance

This book is dedicated to those I've come to know through their
involvement with big cats. Thanks to Lynn Culver for her extensive
notes and videotape on cougar development; Mary Robbins, a fellow
writer and animal lover; Dr. Scott Weldy, the best vet an exotic (or
domestic) could ever have; Brian Werner, the director of Tiger Creek
Wildlife Refuge; and finally to Jeanne Hall, a member of the
Potawatomi tribe, who taught me the true meaning of mountain lion
medicine. Her cougars, Jake, Yamari and Baby, inspired the fictitious
Puma. Jeanne shared every aspect of her life with "the boys."
Without her, the unusual cougar events in this
story wouldn't have been possible.

SILHOUETTE BOOKS

ISBN 0-373-76332-8

NIGHT WIND'S WOMAN

Copyright © 2000 by Sheree Henry-WhiteFeather

Visit Silhouette at www.eHarlequin.com

Printed in U.S.A.

Books by Sheri WhiteFeather

Silhouette Desire

Warrior's Baby #1248
Skyler Hawk: Lone Brave #1272
Jesse Hawk: Brave Father #1278
Cheyenne Dad #1300
Night Wind's Woman #1332

SHERI WHITEFEATHER

lives in Southern California and enjoys ethnic dining, summer powwows and visiting art galleries and vintage clothing stores near the beach. Since her one true passion is writing, she is thrilled to be a part of the Silhouette Desire line. When she isn't writing, she often reads until the wee hours of the morning.

Sheri also works as a leather artisan with her Muscogee Creek husband. They have one son and a menagerie of pets, including a pampered English bulldog and four equally spoiled Bengal cats. She would love to hear from her readers. You may write to her at: P.O. Box 5130, Orange, California 92863-5130.

IT'S OUR 20th ANNIVERSARY!
We'll be celebrating all year,
Continuing with these fabulous titles,
On sale in November 2000.

Desire

#1327 Marriage Prey
Annette Broadrick

#1328 Her Perfect Man
Mary Lynn Baxter

#1329 A Cowboy's Gift
Anne McAllister

#1330 Husband—or Enemy?
Caroline Cross

#1331 The Virgin and the Vengeful Groom
Dixie Browning

#1332 Night Wind's Woman
Sheri WhiteFeather

Romance

#1480 Her Honor-Bound Lawman
Karen Rose Smith

#1481 Raffling Ryan
Kasey Michaels

#1482 The Millionaire's Waitress Wife
Carolyn Zane

#1483 The Doctor's Medicine Woman
Donna Clayton

#1484 The Third Kiss
Leanna Wilson

#1485 The Wedding Lullaby
Melissa McClone

Special Edition

#1357 A Man Alone
Lindsay McKenna

#1358 The Rancher Next Door
Susan Mallery

#1359 Sophie's Scandal
Penny Richards

#1360 The Bridal Quest
Jennifer Mikels

#1361 Baby of Convenience
Diana Whitney

#1362 Just Eight Months Old...
Tori Carrington

Intimate Moments

#1039 The Brands Who Came for Christmas
Maggie Shayne

#1040 Hero at Large
Robyn Amos

#1041 Made for Each Other
Doreen Owens Malek

#1042 Hero for Hire
Marie Ferrarella

#1043 Dangerous Liaisons
Maggie Price

#1044 Dad in Blue
Shelley Cooper

One

Kelly Baxter waited at her neighbor's door, miles of West Texas surrounding her. During the long, dusty ride, she had driven past cattle ranches and crooked wood fencing, abandoned trucks and fields of bluebonnets. And now she stood on the front porch of a large country house, sidestepping an arrangement of potted plants and sun-bleached cow skulls.

The Western charm hadn't eased her frazzled nerves. She had argued with her mother about making this trip. "You shouldn't be traveling alone," her mom had said, "and you shouldn't stay in some run-down, old cabin in the middle of nowhere, either. Not when you have a paternity suit to consider."

Kelly rested her hand on her protruding tummy. She had inherited the cabin from her grandpa and, at this particular time in her life, the middle of nowhere suited her just fine. But to appease her mom, she promised to stop by Dr. McKinley's, the neighbor Grandpa had considered a friend. She would introduce herself, then be on her way.

When the front door finally opened, she could only stare. The man on the other side wasn't Dr. McKinley. He was much too young and much too dark to fit Grandpa's description of the fifty-some-year-old veterinarian.

"I'm Kelly Baxter," she said hastily. "And you must be Shane Night Wind." The doctor's half-Comanche son, the man Grandpa had deemed "part wildcat."

"Kelly Baxter?"

He returned her stare with a deeply-fixed gaze, brown eyes shimmering with tiny flecks of gold. Those eyes scanned the length of her, settling momentarily on her protruding tummy.

She studied his posture: the long, rangy stillness, the muscles waiting to bunch. She took a step back. "Is Dr. McKinley here?" she asked, anxious to exchange the son for the father. Supposedly Tom McKinley had a friendly grin and Irish red hair. Shane's dark mane fell beyond his shoulders, and his lips bore not even the slightest trace of a smile.

"He's out on a ranch call. May I help you?"

"I just stopped by to introduce myself. I'm Butch's granddaughter. I'll be staying at the cabin for a few weeks. I'm on my way there now."

Recognition, then sorrow swept across his face. "Butch was a good man, Miz Baxter. I'm sorry you lost him."

"Thank you."

Her kind-spirited grandpa, an Ohio factory worker, had died ten months before. He had vacationed regularly at a rustic Texas cabin, the place where he had hoped to spend his retirement—a long-awaited dream that never came true. Lung cancer had claimed him instead.

Kelly took a deep breath. She missed him even more now. He would have understood her indecision concerning the baby, the uncertainty about embarking on a paternity suit. And he would have hugged her pain away, the ache that never left her heart.

Shane's gaze dropped to her stomach again. "Is someone meeting you at the cabin?"

"No, I'm..." She lifted her chin, unnerved by his presumption. "I came here on my own."

"You're alone?" He shook his head. "I'm sorry, Miz Baxter, but do you realize how far from town we are?"

Kelly fisted her hands, defiance surging into her weary bones. Her mother had said nearly the same thing. Grandpa's cabin was too far from civilization. It wasn't safe. She needed to stay home and face her situation. Running away wasn't going to help.

Shane stepped forward, and Kelly narrowed her eyes. If his next words sounded anything remotely similar to "this is no place for a pregnant woman," she just might have to deck him or, at least, give it her best shot. Her doctor had given her a clean bill of health, suggesting a routine appointment upon her return. The cabin was going to be her sanctuary, a quiet place to escape, if only for a few short weeks.

She squared her shoulders. "I should go." She had endured a long, turbulent plane ride and even longer, bumpier roads only to come face-to-face with disapproval from a complete stranger. She met with plenty of opposition at home, more than enough. Shane Night Wind she could do without.

"Wait." As she turned to leave, he reached for her arm, brushing her skin.

She met his gaze. The gold in his eyes had deepened.

"That cabin has been vacant for over a year."

Kelly swallowed. Decking him had been a ridiculous thought. This man in frayed blue jeans and scuffed leather boots towered over her by at least a foot. "I called ahead to the realty company Grandpa had used. They assured me the phone and utilities would be in working order."

Rather than respond, he slid his gaze over her body. He couldn't seem to take his eyes off her tummy, she noticed. And he had yet to smile. The combination made her more than uncomfortable. Maybe it was the "wildcat" in him, the dark windblown hair, the primitive sound of his voice, the slow drawl, the cautious way in which he moved, tilted his head. Then again, how dangerous could a man be who took in strays? Somewhere beyond her neighbor's fence was an exotic feline refuge—a rescue for abandoned and abused animals.

Carnivorous animals, she reminded herself. Big, restless cats who stalked their prey.

This time when Kelly turned to leave, he didn't stop her. "It's time for me to go," she said, anxious to escape. Kelly Baxter had come to Texas to be alone.

Three hours later Shane sat on the porch steps waiting for his dad. He had plenty to do, but couldn't bring himself to confront the paperwork that faced him. Ledgers, bills. He wasn't in the mood to find out what he already knew. Soon it would be time to plan another fund-raiser, the social functions he detested.

Yeah, right, a voice in his head said. It wasn't the impending fund-raiser that had him feeling so damn edgy. It was the woman. The *pregnant* woman. The one who'd darted off like a cottontail in the scope of a .22. He'd made her as uncomfortable as she'd made him.

As his father's dually rolled onto the graveled driveway, Shane breathed a sigh of relief. He had to get Kelly Baxter off his chest.

Tom exited his vehicle, his ruddy face alight with a smile. How different they were, Shane thought. Father and son. Men who had been strangers not more than five years before.

Tom stepped onto the porch and ruffled his son's hair. It was a gesture more fitting of the father of a six-year-old, but Shane let the affection pass without ducking his head. Tom probably used to do that to Danny, the half-brother Shane had never known.

He glanced up. Tom stood tall and broad, his shoulders blocking the sun. Shane had inherited his father's stature, but that was where the similarity ended.

"Butch Baxter's granddaughter stopped by today," he said finally.

Tom dropped onto the porch steps. "Really? Is she here to sell the cabin?"

"Maybe. I'm not sure. She plans on staying for a couple of weeks."

"Her name's Kelly, isn't it? Butch used to mention her quite a bit."

Shane squinted into the setting sun. Trust his dad to remember the name of a girl he had never met. Even though Butch only stayed in the cabin for a few months out of the year, Tom and the older man had become friends.

"She came out here by herself, Dad."

"Butch said she was independent. Besides, she's a grown woman."

"I suppose." Wheat-colored hair with a scatter of freckles just below the surface of her skin. She had looked more like a girl than a woman. Defiant one minute, vulnerable the next.

Tom turned his head. "What is it you're not telling me?"

"Nothing."

"Shane?" A scolding tone edged the other man's voice.

"She's pregnant." He clasped his hands together and held them away from his body. "Out-to-here pregnant."

"Oh, I see." Tom dragged a hand through his carrot-topped hair.

Shane knew his father didn't know what else to say. That part of Shane's life was supposed to be closed, the wound healed.

Suddenly he wanted to cry, paint his face and cut his skin. Mourn his loss the Comanche way, a loss that had become another man's gain. Five years had gone by, and now Kelly Baxter had brought every ounce of that old pain screeching back. The betrayal, the anger, the anxiety, the hope—the riot of emotions.

Why did she trigger reminders of the past? Was it the sadness he saw in her eyes? The loneliness?

Shane glanced at the fence that separated his home from the rescue. Deep down he knew. Something was desperately wrong in Kelly Baxter's life, the way it had been wrong in his.

"Why would a woman nearing childbirth want to stay in a cabin by herself?"

"I don't know." Tom looked directly into his son's eyes. "But maybe you better forget about her. Let her live her life and you live yours. You don't need to get tangled up in her affairs."

So Kelly had stirred all those old, painful memories. So what? Shane knew better than to get overly involved. "She's only going to be here for a few weeks. Come on, Dad, it's not like I'm going to get attached. I'm just concerned about a neighbor, that's all."

"You're right, I'm sorry. She's all by herself. I'm sure she could use a friend. Tell her I'd like to meet her."

Shane raised an eyebrow, and Tom smiled. "Don't pretend you weren't thinking about heading over to the cabin to see her. It's written all over your face, son."

He returned the smile and reached into his pocket for his truck keys. His father had come to know him well. The cabin was exactly where he intended to go.

When the small log dwelling came into view, he noticed the trees surrounding it had grown fuller, providing ample shade and pleasant greenery. But the rustic beauty didn't fool him. Even though the cabin contained indoor plumbing and a small but functional kitchen, it was, in Shane's opinion, as crude as cowboy carpentry could get. Too primitive for a pregnant Ohio waif. Her granddaddy had been made of stronger stuff.

Was she married? he wondered. The fact that she'd introduced herself as Kelly Baxter didn't mean she didn't have a husband. Some women kept their maiden names. He stood beside the truck, debating on whether to proceed. Another man's wife should be that other man's concern, not his.

Shane dug his heel into the dirt. If she had a husband, then the guy was a jerk for letting her run off alone like she had. A pregnant woman wouldn't take refuge in a remote Texas cabin over some frivolous marital tiff. Whatever plagued Kelly Baxter was serious.

He couldn't walk away. He just couldn't.

Rather than knock on the open door, he entered the cabin and turned toward the tiny kitchen. He could feel her there, knew she would be hovering over the sink, scrubbing the stained porcelain. He didn't stop to wonder how he knew; he wasn't the sort of man to analyze what some people referred to as a sixth sense. Shane Night Wind had accepted himself as the cougar he'd become.

Although the furniture was still draped with sheets, the cabin wore a layer of dust, cobwebs collecting in every corner. They clung to the beams, sticky against the wood. He hated that feeling, the sensation of being trapped in a web. He assumed she did, too. The kitchen corners had already been brushed clean, the clay-tiled floor swept.

Kelly stood at the sink, running water that was probably spitting rust. She had pinned her hair up, he noticed, clipped it with a metal barrette. Some of it had fallen loose, blond and flyaway. Her hair was nearly as long as his, but it appeared soft and light, almost feathery. From the back she didn't look pregnant. She had an urchin's body, small and frail, her wrinkled cotton dress giving the false illusion of being a size too big.

She turned, caught sight of him and gasped. "What are you doing here?" Water dripped from the sponge in her hand, running down her wrist.

He imagined her heart had lunged for her throat, and he cursed himself for invading her privacy, for not having the good sense to knock. She was afraid of him—the man and the cougar. Both sides of him made her uneasy.

"I'm sorry, I didn't mean to startle you. I just wanted to see if you were okay. If you needed any help getting settled."

She dropped the sponge into the sink and dried her hands on a paper towel. Exhaling an audible breath, she met his gaze. "I hadn't realized how dirty this place would be. I assumed the realtor would have taken care of it. When I called to complain, the receptionist apologized, but said they couldn't get someone out here for at least two days."

He motioned to the cleaning supplies littering the counter. "Looks like you came prepared anyway."

"Hardly. I went down to that little corner store and bought all this stuff."

Shane nodded. The One Stop was a two-pump gas station and minimart, overpriced and under stocked. Cities had those kind of places, too—convenience chains that got robbed in the middle of the night. Of course the One Stop had never been robbed, but then Barry Hunt told anyone who would listen that he kept a sawed-off shotgun beneath the counter.

"So you met Barry," he said.

She flashed an amused smile. "If you mean that nosy old codger with the wad of tobacco in his mouth, then yes, I met him. He's quite a character."

Shane returned her smile. Barry Hunt did poke his bulbous nose into everyone's business. He cussed like a sailor too long at sea, looked like a salty old miner and gossiped with the gusto of a matron at a church social. Everyone from here to the next county would soon know that a pregnant waif named Kelly Baxter was staying in her granddaddy's cabin. Shane dropped his smile, feeling suddenly protective of the urchin and her unborn child. Abused and abandoned creatures had become the focus of his life.

But not married women, he told himself a moment later.

"Does your husband know you're here, Miz Baxter?"

She flinched, his direct question catching her off guard. "No. I mean, I'm not—" She placed her hand on her stomach in what seemed like an unconscious and naturally maternal gesture. "I'm not married, but I have a mother and she knows I'm here."

The part about her mother sounded almost like a warning, as if Mom would call out the national guard if Kelly didn't make a nightly phone call.

She was still unsure of him, he realized, still wary. And no wonder. He hadn't been exactly neighborly on the porch. But opening the door and seeing her standing there had spun him back in time—to the most painful era of his life.

"I can help clean," he offered. "Maybe tackle the bathroom."

"Thank you, but that's not necessary."

"I used to live here," he said, gauging her reaction. Clearly Kelly Baxter couldn't fathom having him scrub her bathroom, the place where she would shower, comb her hair, smooth lotion on her skin. "I know this cabin pretty well."

She leaned against the sink. "Grandpa bought this place from some people by the name of Mendoza."

"Yeah, I know. I worked for the Mendozas. They offered me room and board in exchange for some repairs and construction work that needed done at the rescue. Of course they paid me a small wage, too." Shane paused, realizing he'd made himself sound like some sort of drifter. But explaining why he left a good paying job and nice suburban home in Oklahoma to live in a crude Texas cabin wasn't possible. It would mean mentioning Tami. And the baby.

Kelly stood watching him, so he continued, leaving deliberate gaps. "To make a long story short, Dad and I eventually took over the rescue from the Mendozas. We bought their house and most of their acreage, too. But we didn't really need the cabin and couldn't afford the extra land, so they sold it to your Grandpa instead."

"Grandpa was fascinated with the rescue," Kelly said, looking a tad more comfortable. "He liked the idea of having lions and tigers for neighbors."

"That was a relief to the Mendozas. They were worried about being able to sell the cabin. Most folks don't cotton to big cats the way your granddaddy did." Shane found himself wondering what Kelly thought about sleeping only a few miles away from the wild creatures that shared his life. The animals that had led him to his father, helped him overcome the pain of leaving a wife and child behind.

When their conversation faltered, he convinced Kelly to accept his offer to scour the bathroom. He couldn't imagine her leaning over the tub in her condition. She was all baby, he thought, a tiny girl with a huge tummy.

He walked into the bathroom and winced. A thin layer of dust had settled everywhere, not to mention a few active webs. Men weren't supposed to be afraid of spiders, but arachnophobia had surfaced during childhood. He'd rather enter a lion's den any day.

An hour later with dead spiders in his wake and sweat beading his brow, he returned to the kitchen to see if Kelly had a cold drink available. It appeared the cabin still didn't have a swamp cooler.

He found her sitting at the battered oak table, her face pale. "Are you okay?"

"Just a bit tired," she answered, her voice weary. "It's been a long day."

Too long for a woman carrying a child, he realized. Shane moved closer. "When's your baby due?"

She held a wet cloth against her neck. "Next month, around the twenty-eighth."

He wanted to reprimand her again, but couldn't get past her fragility. He had been through Tami's pregnancy, knew the toll the last trimester took on a woman's body. "You can't push yourself like this, Miz Baxter. You shouldn't be cleaning this old place."

"I hadn't intended to."

"I know." He sat across from her. "Why don't you stay with my dad and me until the realtor can get a cleaning crew out here? There's too much that needs done, and you can't sleep in all this dust."

"That's very kind of you, but maybe I should get a motel room instead."

"The nearest motel is in town and that's a good distance from here. Besides, it's a fleabag. Nobody but truckers bunk there." Truckers and drunken cowboys cheating on their women. This little waif didn't belong in that environment.

Apparently too tired to argue, she moved the cloth to her forehead and accepted his offer. "Grandpa said your dad was a nice man. I think Grandpa would have approved of me staying at your place. And truthfully, all these cobwebs are making me jumpy."

The cobwebs were making Shane jumpy, too, but he wasn't about to admit it. "Yeah, Butch and my dad were pretty good friends," he responded, wondering what her granddaddy had said about him. What had Butch Baxter told Kelly about the veterinarian's Comanche son? "I hope you don't mind eating breakfast for dinner. I think Dad plans on frying up some eggs and potatoes. It's his turn to cook."

"That sounds fine. Thank you. I don't know what I would have done without you."

"Just being neighborly." He resisted the urge to place his hand against her tummy, take comfort in the warmth. Even though the chemical smell of a household cleanser lingered on her hands, he still detected another scent. Watermelon. A gently milled soap or body lotion.

What would she do if he actually touched her?

Nothing, he decided. Most pregnant women became accustomed to forms of affection from strangers. Affection? The last thing he needed was to feel something for her. She was carrying another man's child. Just like Tami had been.

Shane cursed his memories. Tami hadn't liked her body then, but he had enjoyed the fullness, knowing a child grew there. He shifted his gaze. A child he had been denied.

"Come on, Miz Baxter, let's get going."

She rose, her skin still pale. "If we're going to be friends, then call me Kelly, please."

He nodded, wondering what the hell he was doing. The last woman who had claimed to be his friend had gashed his heart. And now this delicate-looking urchin with the flyaway hair and spray of golden freckles managed to show up at his door and reopen that wound.

Five years of living like a cougar had only reinforced one thing. The man in Shane still remembered what it felt like to hurt.

Kelly walked into Shane's home, deciding fatigue was her enemy. She had just agreed to spend two days with two men she barely knew. Barely knew? She hadn't even met Dr. Mc-Kinley yet.

"Come on, I'll introduce you to my dad," Shane said as though reading her mind.

Kelly followed her neighbor to a brightly lit kitchen. The stove was old but clean, the counters butcher-block style. The house boasted masculine charm, simple and stark with polished wood floors and heavy rattan furniture.

"Dad, I've got somebody with me."

Tom McKinley turned. He was as tall as Shane and possibly as muscular, but his features weren't as sharp as his son's, and his eyes weren't flecked with gold. They were pale blue, a complement to his sunburned skin and thick red hair. Tom had a nonthreatening appearance, whereas Shane had the kind of dark, dangerous looks that probably made women stop and stare. Kelly glanced away. Even she had stared a little.

"This is Kelly Baxter, Butch's granddaughter."

Upon hearing her name, she steadied her gaze and extended her hand to Dr. McKinley, realizing an introduction was being made.

The veterinarian shook her hand, then gave it a paternal pat. "You're as pretty as your granddaddy said."

"Thank you."

Shane explained her dilemma, and Dr. McKinley welcomed her to their home with a genuine smile. How warm their relationship was, she thought, how calm. Nothing like the recent disagreements that existed between herself and her mother. Those disagreements had brought her to Texas, that and the pain of a man's rejection.

The doctor went back to preparing supper, and Shane led her down the hallway, her luggage in tow. He offered Kelly a friendly smile—the polite, gallant host. An enigma, she thought, his renegade looks deceiving.

"You can sleep in here," he said as they entered a tidy little guest room.

The first thing Kelly noticed was the tall, metal cage. Inside of it was a spotted cat, surrounded by toys and snug in a padded box, its huge ears perked with curiosity.

Shane set her bags on the floor and moved toward the cage. "That's Zuni. I hope you don't mind sharing your space with her. She's more or less a houseguest, too." He knelt to slip a finger through the bars. The cat poked her paw back at him. "You know, come to think of it, I better move Zuni into my room. We're still bottle-feeding her. I doubt you'd appreciate being awakened every four hours."

"She's still a baby?" Zuni was already half the size of a full-grown domestic, fine-boned and adorable. "How old is she?"

"Five weeks."

Shane opened the cage and the kitten scampered out, rubbing and purring between his legs. "She's a serval. A medium-size cat from Africa." He reached for a toy and shook it in front of Zuni. The kitten batted it immediately. "But this little girl was born in captivity. She's never been to Africa."

"Is she a rescue?" Kelly wanted to snag Zuni and cuddle, but wasn't sure if it would be the proper thing to do.

He shook his head. "Kittens and cubs rarely need rescuing. Everyone adores baby animals. It's when they get big that they become a problem. Zuni belongs to a friend of mine, and he's prepared for the handful she's going to become. I'm only baby-sitting while he's on vacation."

Shane looked up from the kitten and smiled. Kelly assumed she had a sappy look on her face, the expression of an expectant mother eager to nuzzle someone else's toddler. Shane appeared amused. "Do you want to hold her?"

He didn't need to ask twice. Kelly extended her arms and waited for the transfer. The kitten had soft, fluffy fur and long, spindly legs. Her little nose was pointed, her eyes round and dark. It was thrilling, Kelly thought, to stroke an exotic creature, listen to the low rumble of its purr.

"Do you think you could teach me to feed her? I'm willing to get up every four hours. It's something I'm going to have to get used to anyway."

"Are you sure?" he asked.

She brought the kitten closer. "Positive"

Ten minutes later Kelly had been instructed on how to mix the formula and warm the bottle. She stood beside Shane in the kitchen while his father peeled a batch of potatoes.

Shane handed Kelly the bottle. "We're a little off schedule, but I'm sure Zuni won't mind."

She glanced at Tom McKinley. He sent her a smile, then looked over at his son. He was proud of Shane, she thought. Father and son treated each other with respect. Did they ever argue? she wondered. Kelly and her mother used to get along well, too. But the paternity suit issue had caused a rift between them.

Shane and Kelly returned to the guest room where the kitten had been left to roam. The moment Zuni spotted the bottle, she sat at Kelly's feet and made a noise that sounded as if it had come from a bird, an odd little chirping.

"That's the most common way servals communicate," Shane explained. "Not all cats roar or meow."

They settled on the edge of the bed, Zuni climbing onto Kelly's lap, anxious and jittery for her meal. Shane leaned in close, and Kelly swallowed. Suddenly his presence seemed too intimate. The bedroom door was closed, the lamp turned low.

"Feed her as though she's nursing from her mother," he said quietly. "Keep her on her tummy and guide her head. Cats aren't like human babies. You shouldn't cradle them while they're eating. They can get milk in their lungs."

Kelly listened to his instruction and watched Zuni latch onto the nipple. The kitten's ears drew back as she suckled, her round eyes slitting languorously.

Shane slipped his arm around Kelly and readjusted the bottle. "You need to give her something to knead. See how she's trying to find a place for her paws? Let her use your hand."

Kelly nodded. Did Shane realize how close he was? That his breath stirred against her cheek?

The sound of Zuni's suckling intensified the quiet. Shane kept his arm draped across her shoulder, his gaze focused on the kitten. She had the sudden urge to lean into him, absorb his kindness. She had dreamed of moments like this. The players were wrong, but the feeling was right. The tender stillness. The human warmth.

Zuni released the nipple, gazed up at Kelly, then latched onto the rubber again and began to chew.

Shane wiggled the bottle. "No, no, little one. This isn't playtime."

He lifted his arm from Kelly's shoulder. She felt an immediate loss. The spell had been broken, reality creeping back in. Shane wasn't Jason. He wasn't the father of her child, the man who should be treating her with kindness.

After turning the light up, Shane took the bottle and charted the amount the kitten had consumed. He appeared to be a nice person, but then Jason had fooled her into believing he was nice, too. Unlike Shane, her baby's father wasn't long and lean, nor did he wear frayed denims and scuffed leather boots. Jason Collier had neatly styled hair, his features classically handsome, his medium build well-suited to collegiate-type sportswear. He had been her romantic fixation since high school, the popular boy most folks in her hometown seemed to like.

"Zuni needs to be burped."

"What?" She blinked away her thoughts, then glanced down at the squirming kitten. "How—"

"Just lift her onto your shoulder and pat."

"Like a baby?"

Shane nodded and returned to Kelly's side. She raised the kitten. "I can't believe I'm burping a cat."

"I can't believe she hasn't tried to nip you." He placed his fingers over Kelly's and urged her to continue the gentle tapping. "Servals tend to be nippy. Mostly it's just play-biting but, regardless, it can hurt." He stroked the kitten's head. "Disciplining this little girl isn't going to be easy."

When Zuni erupted in a loud burp Kelly looked at Shane, and they both laughed.

"I guess she told you."

"Yeah. I guess she did." He grinned, then smoothed a strand of Kelly's hair, removing it from Zuni's curious reach.

That tender sensation came back, the unspoken compatibility. Kelly released a slow steadying breath and pushed away the feeling. In two weeks she would return to Ohio to face an important decision in her life. A decision that didn't include Shane Night Wind.

Two

Shane hadn't slept well. He had tossed and turned, wondering about Kelly Baxter. The same thought still plagued him: Why had she come to Texas to spend two weeks in her granddaddy's cabin a month before her baby was due? That made no sense.

They had shared dinner last night with his father, but the conversation hadn't led to any clues. Her personal life hadn't been broached.

Strange how Shane wanted to be near her, yet her presence stirred such raw emotion within him—painful reminders of the past. The turbulent years between Shane and his father. The bitterness in Shane's childhood. The wife and baby he had been forced to leave behind. The wife and son Tom had lost.

Kelly Baxter had brought a battered suitcase of ghosts with her—haunting memories Shane had struggled to overcome.

He poured a cup of freshly brewed coffee. It wasn't Kelly's fault, the emotions swirling around inside him. She hadn't come to Texas to torment him. She had come out of her own torment.

Maybe, just maybe, he thought, he was meant to help her. Maybe the Creator had placed her in his path for a reason. It was possible his own pain had resurfaced as a reminder of what it felt like to be needy and alone—the way Kelly appeared to be.

Shane sipped his coffee, suddenly sensing Kelly's impending presence. He could feel another person approaching and knew it wasn't his dad. Tom had left for work already.

She appeared in the kitchen entryway, sleepy-eyed, her flyaway locks spilling over her shoulders. She wore a modest nightgown that flowed to her ankles. Pretty and pregnant, he thought, wrapped in pink.

"Oh, hi." She smiled a little shyly. "I didn't know anyone would be up at this hour."

"We start our day early around here." Watermelon still lingered on her skin, the same scent he had noticed the day before. Shane moved a little closer. Watermelon was significant in his life, the treat his favorite cougar salivated for. He moistened his lips as a masculine urge took hold. Suddenly he imagined nuzzling her neck, burying his face in her hair.

"I came to get Zuni a bottle," she said.

"Huh? Oh, yeah. There's one in the fridge." Guiltily, he rejected his coffee, thinking caffeine was probably the last thing he needed, especially since his heartbeat had quickened.

So he had romantic urges. So what? He wasn't having full-on sexual fantasies about a pregnant woman, just odd little flutters, feelings that leaned more toward tenderness. The kind of touches that led to cuddling. Kissing.

Kelly turned to warm the bottle, and Shane gave himself a mental lashing. Romantic urges. She was carrying another man's child. Hadn't he learned his lesson from Tami? Been down that painful road before?

Damn. Was it Kelly's pregnancy that drew him in—the overwhelming reminder of a child he still missed? Or was it actually her? The feminine defiance and girlish vulnerability? A combination he found difficult to resist.

It didn't matter, Shane decided. He wasn't about to lose the peace he'd made with himself, not now, not after all he'd been through. If the problem in Kelly's life centered around her baby's father, then he'd find out why. And if it was too serious of a problem to fix, he'd encourage Kelly to move forward, find a new direction to take, focus on her baby, maybe even consider a new career. Start over the way he had.

"Do you want to take a tour of the rescue later?" he asked.

"You don't have to entertain me, Shane. I've taken enough of your time already."

"I'd really like you to see it." And he wanted to get to the bottom of her pain, the reason she'd left home. "It's really incredible. We've spent a lot of time and money building natural habitats, and we even have a picnic area for the tourists."

"Would I be going through the tour with other people?"

"No, just me. We only give scheduled tours on the first Saturday of every month. We just don't have the staff available to offer them more frequently. Besides, the cats deserve their privacy." He tilted his head. "I would never put you in any danger, Kelly. The rescue is safe." And free of the toxoplasmosis that could harm an unborn child. Having a veterinarian in the family kept the strong cats healthy and the ones who required constant medical care well tended. Tom was available day or night, a dedicated doctor who had been treating exotics for years. "Please say yes."

"Okay." She tested the temperature of the formula. "I'd like to see the animals Grandpa found so fascinating."

"Good. We can pack a lunch. Spend some time in the shade." And talk, he hoped. Once he helped Kelly sort out her problems, he could go back to his own life. The solitude he had come to rely on.

Hours later Kelly walked beside Shane, thoroughly enjoying the outdoors. Jungle Hill Rescue was a sight to behold. Spring greenery flourished beneath a vast Texas sky, and wide dirt paths led to large caged compounds.

"Most of our residents are cougars," he said. "But we have other cats, too." He guided her toward a grassy compound where a tiger peered down at the world from a tree house, its sleek body stretched across the bark. "We don't pick and choose our animals. We take them in with the intention to keep them, regardless of their health or disposition. We're not a temporary shelter." He turned to gaze up at the tiger. "Once they arrive, this is their permanent home. Their last stop."

Kelly studied Shane's profile. The inflection in his voice spoke of sadness, as if he understood the feeling of being homeless, of needing a caring place to live. "So they've been abused?" she asked.

"Not all of them." He shifted the backpack that contained their lunch. "Some are more or less orphaned. Think about it, if a primary caregiver dies, who is going to take in their three-hundred-pound cat? It's a misconception that all of the animals in rescues have been abused or purposely abandoned. There are some responsible private owners out there. We've acquired our exotics from all sorts of situations. Unfortunately, though, some of those situations were deplorable."

"I can't imagine having a big cat for a pet."

He turned to look at her, his brown eyes glinting gold. "That's because they're not pets. It's not the same as owning a dog or a domestic cat."

Kelly understood what he meant. The people who purchased exotics and expected them to behave like domestics were the ones who ultimately ended up abusing or abandoning their animals, realizing the nature of the beast much too late.

"You really love them."

He smiled. "Yeah, I do. I feel like I belong to them somehow."

Because he was one of them, Kelly thought, as his hair blew around his shoulders. Long, lean, golden-eyed Shane. Part Comanche, part Irish, part wildcat.

"Tell me about the tiger," she said, deciding she liked her

host. Kelly didn't have many male friends, especially men who wore their hair longer than her own. It was difficult not to find him fascinating.

"That's Sammy." Shane observed the big cat as though pleased by its royal disposition, its ability to accept their presence without swishing its tail or batting an eye. Although they stood a good distance from the spacious habitat, the tiger watched them through a regal gaze—a prince looking down on the peasants. "He came from a tiger mill. Tigers breed easily in captivity, and the demand for white tigers has created a problem. The only known white tiger gene came from a male in India that was bred to his daughter, so the lines aren't pure."

Shane sighed, the sound rough and masculine. "Sammy's an orange tiger who carries the white gene, the product of a breeder trying to capitalize on producing white tigers. When a white tiger is bred to an orange one, the litter is often mixed. So you see, Sammy's immune system isn't what it should be. Besides the gene he carries, we think he was a result from even more inbreeding. An irresponsible mill who mated relatives."

"That's sad."

"Yes, it is. And Sammy's not the only discarded tiger out there. I know of rescues that are filled with them." Shane moved his gaze over Kelly's body. "Are you doing all right? Do you want to sit down for a while?"

Startled by his quick change of subject, she smoothed her windblown hair, feeling suddenly fat and unattractive. It bothered her that his gaze always managed to stray to her protruding belly. She had the sensation that her pregnancy made him uncomfortable, that he found her added weight an unwelcome distraction. "Why? Do I look tired?"

He swallowed, his Adam's apple bobbing. "No. It's just that once I start talking about the cats, I lose track of time. And you're…you know…"

Pregnant, she added silently, wondering why he had trouble saying the word. Maybe it was the bachelor in him, the single, childless male. Jason had trouble with the word, too. And the image. The father of her baby didn't want to be a father.

"Why don't we have lunch and finish the tour afterward?" he suggested.

"Okay." In truth, she was actually ready for a break. Swollen feet and backaches came more regularly these days, the baby in her womb growing rapidly.

The picnic area was located just outside the rescue. Wooden benches provided rough-hewn seating and ancient oaks offered shelter from the dusty winds. She found the parklike setting appealing, especially since beyond the chain-link fence were endless miles of uncultivated land. Shane's property sat on a small hillside, overlooking the plains. The wide-open space gave her a sense of freedom.

"What's that building?" she asked, referring to a large tiki-type hut.

"It's going to be our gift shop. We just haven't had the chance to stock it yet. We plan on having some T-shirts made. Coffee cups, too. You know, things that promote the rescue. We survive on donations and membership support."

She took in her surroundings once again. "I really like it here."

He smiled and unpacked their food. "Yeah, me, too."

They had chosen to make a simple lunch: turkey sandwiches, cheese-flavored crackers, apples and bottled water. Everything in Duarte seemed simple to Kelly, at least all that she had seen so far. She hadn't been to town yet, but remembered that Grandpa had described it as a secluded corner of Texas, as old-fashioned as a blue-chip stamp, a place where time stood still.

Kelly reached for her water. Time was just what she needed. Time to be alone, to think and make decisions. Being far from home helped, knowing that she didn't have to argue with her mother or obsess about Jason's return from his business travels—a trip she believed he had scheduled to avoid her.

"So what's your hometown like?" Shane asked.

She glanced down at her sandwich. Strange how he always

managed to tap into her thoughts. "It's a nice place. A small suburban town where most of us know each other." Kelly had been born in Tannery, Ohio, attended school there, sold Girl Scout cookies, landed her first and only job, buried Grandpa in the hilltop cemetery. It was home, yet she didn't want to be there. Not now.

"So you're a grocery checker, right?" he asked.

Kelly nodded. She had told him what she did for a living the previous evening over supper. "The pay is pretty good, and I've got excellent health benefits."

He studied his apple, then buffed it against his shirt. "Yeah, but it's not right for you."

She wasn't sure if she should take offense. No one had ever questioned her job before. "I like talking to the customers, seeing the people I grew up around."

He met her gaze, the polished apple gleaming in his hand. "Yeah, but there's more to you than that. There's something you have a passion for. I can feel it, even see it in your eyes."

A shiver worked its way up her spine. Being held within his stare was unnerving. Soul-piercing, she decided, like being stalked by a mountain lion. And she did have a passion. Nothing glamorous, just a quiet hobby. She liked to draw. Just for herself, pictures of plants and animals—her mother's garden, a neighbor's puppy, things that made her feel good. But even so, she wasn't foolhardy enough to believe her drawings would please anyone but herself.

"I'm fine with my job," she said, even though she wasn't. Nothing was fine in her life. Nothing. Rather than look forward to becoming a grandmother, Kelly's mother had turned the welfare of Kelly's child into a lawsuit. And Jason? His bitter feelings hurt most of all. One minute he insisted the baby wasn't his, and the next he accused Kelly of getting pregnant on purpose.

Shane continued to stare into her eyes, his voice gentle. "If you feel like talking about it, I want you to know I'm here. I'm a good listener."

Kelly tore at the crust on her sandwich. "Am I that obvious?"

"You're all alone in Texas a month before your baby is due. That in itself says something."

Suddenly she wanted to cry. She needed a friend, someone who wasn't close to her situation. But could she tell Shane about Jason? About how much his rejection hurt? Or how inadequate she had been as a lover?

"I'm happy about the baby," she said. A little scared about being a single parent, but grateful that God had given her a child. "I appreciate your concern. But I'm going to be fine." She couldn't imagine talking to Shane about Jason. Especially about all the awful things Jason had said to her. The personal, humiliating things.

Shane wondered what to do now. Kelly looked like a lost little girl, an urchin trying to act brave. "How old are you?" he asked.

"Twenty-four."

He took a deep breath. The same age he had been when Tami had become pregnant. "I'm thirty," he told her for lack of something better to say.

"Oh." She glanced down at her food.

Great, he thought, awkward conversation. His brilliant plan to help her wasn't working. Should he share something private, something from his past? Would that encourage her to open up?

Shane bit into the apple. He couldn't tell her about Tami. That was too personal. Admitting that his wife had found him lacking as a husband wasn't something he cared to admit. Tami wouldn't have slept with another man if Shane had satisfied her.

Pushing Tami out of his mind, he decided to test the waters, determine if Kelly's pain was centered around her baby's father. He knew firsthand about reluctant fathers. "I just got acquainted with my dad five years ago."

"Really?" She scooted forward.

"Yeah." He wondered how to tell this story without making Tom seem like the bad guy. Making fathers look bad wasn't the idea, especially if the guy who had made Kelly pregnant was shirking his responsibility. Although the fear of fatherhood hit some men harder than others, Shane believed most guys eventually came around.

"My parents had this sort of casual affair, I guess," he began. "They met in Oklahoma. My dad was from Texas, but he was in school at the time, attending the veterinary college in Stillwater." Shane could see that he'd captured Kelly's attention, so he continued. "Anyway, they ended up sleeping together, and my mom got pregnant."

This, he decided, was where the story got complicated. "But my mom didn't tell Tom about me. And she refused to tell my grandma where Tom could be found. She was afraid Grandma would try to force them into getting married."

"Your mother sounds like an independent woman."

"Yeah. She doesn't believe in loveless marriages, people getting together for the sake of a baby. Of course my traditional grandma saw things differently."

Kelly watched him through interested eyes. "So what happened?"

"By the time Grandma tracked down my dad, I was almost a year old. And Tom…well…he was married to someone else by then." Shane knew it was odd for a son to refer to his father by his given name, but Tom had been a stranger long before Shane had ever called him Dad. "Not only that, but Tom's wife was pregnant. He was about to become a father for the second time."

"Oh, my." Kelly's jaw dropped a little. "It sounds like a soap opera."

"Yeah." He didn't watch daytime TV, but he'd heard how angst-ridden those shows were. "Tom told his wife, and they both agreed that he should take financial responsibility for me. So he sent my mom child support, even though he promised his wife he would never bring me into their lives in any other way."

"And your dad was okay with that?" she asked, uncertainty in her tone.

Apparently Kelly was thinking about the father of her own child. A man Shane had come to wonder about. Had he loved Kelly or had he used her? Had it been a serious relationship or a one-night stand? A hundred scenarios, he realized, were possible. And if Kelly didn't confide in him, he'd probably lay awake that night counting off each and every one.

He discarded his half-eaten apple and answered her question. "Tom felt guilty as hell, but he loved his wife and figured it was the only way to save his marriage."

"What about your mom?"

"She appreciated the child support, especially since she hadn't intended to tell Tom about me in the first place. My grandma was upset, though. Of course there wasn't much she could do about it." Nothing but argue with Shane's mother and insist that Tom had shamed his firstborn by excluding the boy from his life. Shane had been seven years old when he'd first stumbled upon one of those arguments, an innocent second-grader when he'd learned that he had a half brother. A white child his white daddy was raising. Shane's innocence had quickly shattered. He had hated Tom then, hated him with every fiber of his being—a burning that had grown with each passing year.

"You seem close to your dad now," Kelly observed. "He appears to care very deeply about you."

"Tom came to see me when I was eighteen," Shane admitted, "but I told him to go to hell. I didn't want to have anything to do with him." Shame welled in his throat. Shame for hating so deeply, for not recognizing Tom's grief. "His wife and son had just been killed in a plane crash. Emotionally he was a mess."

And Shane's kindhearted, free-spirited mother had reached out to Tom, offering friendship and compassion, something Shane wasn't capable of doing at the time. "I just wanted him to go away. I didn't want to be his instant son, a replacement

for the one he had raised—fair-haired, fair-skinned Danny—
the boy he had really loved.''

Kelly flinched, and Shane realized his voice had taken on
the hurt from his youth. ''I spent over half my life comparing
myself to Danny. Wondering why Tom wanted him over me.
I was bitter and rebellious, but I swear, Kelly, I've come a
long way since then. I don't blame my dad anymore.'' And
he found himself mourning Danny, the brother he had never
known.

''I believe you.'' Her smile was faint but sincere. ''It
couldn't have been easy.''

''No, it wasn't. But neither was Tom losing his wife and
son. Regardless, I avoided my dad for the next seven years. I
didn't see him again until I was twenty-five.''

''Five years ago,'' she remarked, pushing her flyaway hair
out of her eyes.

''Yeah, five years ago.'' Right after he had left Evan behind,
the baby he couldn't keep, the child who wasn't really his.

''What made you decide to get to know your dad then?''
she asked.

''Just some stuff going on in my own life.'' A paternity test
he didn't want to take, a divorce he had tried to stop. Sheer
and utter hell. ''It's over now.''

It had been, he realized, until Kelly Baxter had showed up
at his door. Pregnant, lost little Kelly. He looked across the
table at her. The wind had made a beautiful mess of her hair,
and the sun peeking through the trees highlighted the scatter
of freckles dusting her nose. ''Do you want to finish the
tour?''

''Yes.''

Her voice was as quiet as his, and he decided she wasn't
going to open up, not even after what he'd just told her. But
then, he'd only revealed half of his story. The other half involved his wife and child, the family he had struggled to keep.

Although Kelly and Shane agreed to finish the tour, neither
made a move to leave the bench. They sat silent for a time,

picking at the remainder of their food, each absorbed in their own thoughts. Kelly's strayed to Jason. The story about Shane's parents had triggered an emotional response inside her. Shane's mother hadn't been in love with Tom, but Kelly still had feelings for the father of her child. And now she believed that Jason had only dated her because he enjoyed being admired. Her long-running affection for him was no secret. She had been attracted to Jason since she was a sophomore at Tannery High, and he seemed to thrive on female attention.

And yes, she still had the deep and painful hope that he would take responsibility for his child. Not with money, but with love. She wanted her baby to know its father. If she refused to file the paternity suit her mother was pushing for, would Jason feel less threatened? Less pressured? Would he return from his so-called extended business trip to discuss the welfare of their child?

"Are you ready?" Shane asked.

"Oh, yes. Of course." She discarded her trash in a nearby can. She didn't want to dwell on heartache, especially this afternoon. Shane offered what appeared to be genuine friendship, and she hadn't spent quality time with a friend in ages. Everyone back home was too caught up in the gossip surrounding her and Jason. Would there be a lawsuit? Was she after Jason's money? Had she gotten pregnant on purpose? After all, he was a wealthy young heir and she was just an average middle-class girl.

Kelly placed her hands on her tummy and found herself rewarded with a hearty kick. Comforted by the tiny foot, she smiled. She still had two weeks before she returned to the turmoil surrounding her life. Today she would clear her mind and enjoy the beauty of Texas.

Fifteen minutes later Kelly and Shane stood about four feet from an enclosure that incorporated water, a variety of vegetation and a rocky terrain—a natural habitat. Or as natural as a confined area could be, Shane explained.

The resident was a cougar, an alert, tawny-colored cat. They had looked in on several cougars, but this one, Kelly decided, was different from the rest.

"I wish I could get closer," she said.

Shane unhooked the rope barrier. "With this boy, you can."

As Kelly moved forward, she felt an odd pull toward the animal, a strange affection. Maybe it was the way the big cat moved, the interest he appeared to show. He moved toward the wire fence, then stopped as though anxious for human interaction. Kelly noticed all of the habitats had secondary enclosures attached, a safety precaution, she supposed—a lockdown while the primary pens were being tended.

"Oh." She brought her hand to her heart. The cougar's striking face displayed only one eye.

"Hey, Puma." Shane greeted the cat and received a friendly-sounding *"yaooow"* in return.

Kelly smiled. She assumed the enthusiastic call meant "What's up?" or "How's it going?" in cougar talk. And when Shane mimicked the sound to near perfection, she found herself even more intrigued. A conversation was definitely taking place. But rather than ask what was being said, she posed a more generic question.

"Puma is another word for cougar, isn't it?"

He nodded. "They're considered the cat of many names. Panther, painter, catamount, mountain lion, night screamer, just to name a few."

A small wind kicked up a cloud of dust. "Night screamer?"

"The early explorers used to tell stories about the unearthly screams that came from the mountains." He smiled at Puma. The cat remained at the fence, watching the humans curiously. "Cougars are vocal animals. Besides caterwaul, they hiss and growl. And make mewling sounds. But they don't roar. That's why their babies are referred to as kittens instead of cubs. They're not considered a member of the *Panthera* species, the big cats that have the ability to roar."

"What happened to Puma's eye?"

"It ruptured from something similar to glaucoma. A result

of poor nutrition. He was bottle-fed as a kitten, but the formula was lacking.''

''He's still gorgeous.'' Kelly wanted to sketch the tawny cat, draw the muscular formation of his body, shape of his face, curve of his ears, the exotic flare of his nostrils. She wanted to capture the essence of his nature. What would he feel like? she wondered. ''Do cougars purr?''

Shane's voice took on a slow drawl—a husky, almost lazy quality. ''Yeah, and if you get much closer to the compound, Puma's going to be rumbling up a storm. Salivating, too.''

She took a step back. ''He likes women?''

Shane lowered his head, bringing his mouth close to her ear. His breath was warm, she noticed, as it stirred against her hair.

''Watermelon, Kelly. Puma likes watermelon. Drools all over it before he eats it.''

''Oh.'' A shiver shot up her spine. She had applied her scented body mist liberally that morning, and from the way Shane breathed it in, she assumed he enjoyed watermelon, too.

As he moved back, she decided Shane and Puma seemed like one and the same—two primal creatures. Striking and exotic.

Kelly chewed her bottom lip. Now she wondered if Shane could purr. She studied his profile and noticed the wind seemed to favor his hair. The sun, too. The glossy strands shone with faint auburn highlights. Maybe he could mimic a cougar's rumbling purr. But since her heartbeat had accelerated to a furious pounding, she decided she was better off not knowing.

Three

The cabin had begun to feel like a home. Or a home away from home, Kelly thought. The cleaning crew had done a wonderful job. The rooms reflected pure Western charm. She loved the rough-hewn detail: the beamed ceilings, the stone mantel over the fireplace, the cedar chest filled with Texas trinkets. Since the cabin was so different from her suburban dwelling, she enjoyed the therapy it provided. An old place that felt new—the perfect getaway.

A part of Kelly never wanted to return to Ohio. Of course her home state wasn't the problem. She was still hiding from the decisions that awaited her there. Four days had passed since she'd arrived in Texas, and she wasn't any closer to settling her life.

She sat at the battered dining table, stealing light from a small window. The spring weather had turned gloomy, but that hadn't stopped Kelly from pursuing her current subject. Puma, the one-eyed cougar. She had been sketching pictures of him every morning since she had moved into the cabin.

She couldn't explain her affection for Puma, couldn't quite understand it. Being in the cabin made her feel closer to the tawny-colored cat, something that didn't make much sense.

Drawing from memory wasn't easy for Kelly, in fact she had never done it before. Yet Puma's image filled her mind, even the smallest detail.

A loud knock sounded. Kelly jumped to her feet. She had a pretty good idea who her visitor was. Shane stopped by daily, her gentlemanly neighbor with the slow drawl and worn leather boots. She closed her sketchbook and covered it with a magazine she had found in the cedar chest, then went to open the door.

"Hey, Kelly." A straw cowboy hat shielded his eyes. But not enough, she noticed, to conceal the amber sparkle in them.

A flutter of attraction had her slipping into that flash of gold. The baby kicked just then. A scolding. A reminder that pregnant women shouldn't flirt.

She glanced away. "Come in."

He removed his hat upon entering the cabin, leaving his hair the way it fell. Shane didn't appear to fuss over his appearance. Jason was always groomed to perfection which had her constantly wishing she was prettier and that her body had more curves. Pregnancy fullness didn't count.

Shane set his hat on an end table and placed a plastic animal carrier on the floor. "Zuni wanted to see you."

"She did?" Kelly watched the serval kitten scamper out of the carrier. "Will you pick her up for me? I don't think I can."

"Sure." He lifted Zuni before she darted off. "Guess you're having a little trouble touching your toes these days, huh?"

She appreciated his easy response. It was certainly better than the uncomfortable glances he usually gave her tummy. "Are you kidding?" She motioned to the barrel chair that faced the fireplace. "I can hardly sit without getting stuck."

He eyed the offending chair, then smiled. "It does looks a mite deep. Maybe you better avoid it from here on in."

She returned his casual smile. "So how's my little Zuni?"

He adjusted the kitten with pride. "She learned how to kiss."

"Really?"

"Yep. We've been working on it for days." He moved closer. "Zuni, give Kelly a kissums."

Kissums. Delighted, she leaned forward as Zuni poked her nose out. The kiss resulted in a quick nudge. Kelly squealed and met Shane's gaze over the serval's massive ears. They grinned at each other, smiled happily until the moment turned strangely quiet. They stood inches apart, Shane's arm brushing Kelly's stomach.

The kitten leaped onto the sofa. Kelly wasn't sure what to do or say. Shane didn't move his arm, nor did he step back. Zuni explored the cabin while they faced each other, their gazes locked.

Kelly's mouth went dry. She moistened her lips. Suddenly she wanted to kiss him—gently, with the kind of tenderness she longed to receive from Jason. She didn't want a sexual kiss. She craved comfort, a sensation that would take the hurt away.

A rustling noise caught her attention, but it was Shane who turned away first, breaking their haunting stare. Zuni sat on the dining table, amusing herself with the magazine Kelly had placed over her sketchbook, tearing and crumbling pages.

Shane started toward the kitten before Kelly had the chance. "No, Zuni," he corrected in a stern voice.

Avoiding his reprimand, the serval jumped off the table, sending the magazine and Kelly's sketchbook tumbling to the floor. Shane reached down to right the papers. Kelly stood nearby. Her sketchbook had fallen open, displaying a drawing of Puma.

Embarrassment washed over her. She rarely shared her hobby with anyone. "I was just messing around," she said hastily, wishing she could move fast enough to snatch the booklet off the floor. She had never felt so exposed—naked while being fully clothed.

Shane lifted the drawing to study it. "It's Puma." A breath-taking image of the cougar that had given Shane his heart back, the animal that had lived in his dreams since childhood.

"This is really good." Unnerving, too. The picture could have been him, not in looks but in spirit. Shane had spent years with Puma—pain-cleansing years. He placed the sketch-book on the table. "May I?" he asked Kelly, curious to see her other drawings.

She nodded, then shifted her feet, visibly uncomfortable. "It's just a hobby."

Mesmerized by her hobby, he paged through the booklet, starting with the first sheet. She favored flowers, he noticed, and tall trees—weeping willows draped in beauty and sadness. Another page depicted a puppy, a cute little mutt, the next a row of tomato plants. She had even captured the moisture beading the fruit, making the tomatoes seem red and succulent. He could see rich, vibrant color where there was none.

"Do you paint?" he asked.

"Not really, no."

But she did, he decided. She painted in her mind. He came back to Puma's image. There were four sketches in all, each depicting a different mood. He especially liked the close-up, the one that filled the page, Puma's head lowered in a primal pose. The missing eye didn't detract from the animal's striking appearance. If anything, it added an air of mystery.

Why Puma? Why did she feel compelled to draw his cat? The one that had changed his life? "You spent a lot of time on these pictures." And plenty of passion. He could see it in every line, every dark, primitive shadow. She had breathed life into Puma's sketches. Shane could feel the cougar's sleek fur, even hear the loud hum of his purr. She had captured everything.

Kelly released an audible breath. "I draw almost every morning. I don't drink coffee and I don't jog. So when I wake up early, I take out my sketchbook."

He wanted to ask if he could keep his favorite picture, but

noticed the rendering wasn't quite finished. Apparently he had interrupted her work.

"I feel sort of attached to Puma," she said, her voice shy. "I just keep seeing him in my mind. Every detail."

Images, he realized, that she'd put on paper. "He used to live here."

She cocked her head. "Excuse me?"

"The cougar. Slept here, ate here. Tore up the place a bit." He tried to keep his tone light, even though this whole experience had left him shaken. Kelly Baxter had felt Puma's spirit. Now Shane knew, without a doubt, that he was meant to help her. He scrubbed his hand across his jaw. How could he make a difference in her life in less than two weeks? Kelly still hadn't told him what troubled her.

"A cougar actually lived here?" She leaned forward. "How? I mean why?"

"I was trying to prove something to myself, I guess. And to my dad. I was having some trouble warming up to Tom then. About the only thing we had in common was our interest in big cats."

Kelly sat at the table and looked up at him. "So your dad introduced you to the Mendozas, the people who owned the rescue?"

"Yeah. Tom was their vet. But he didn't get paid. He volunteered his time. Most rescues can't afford to pay a vet, especially since so many of their animals are in poor health when they first arrive. It made me sort of mad that he was so damn noble, but deep down, I respected him for it, too."

Shane seated himself across from Kelly. "Regardless, I was still hurt that my dad had raised his white son instead of me." And Shane was devastated that his Comanche wife had cheated on him with a white man—a wealthy, young lawyer—a man who had claimed the child Shane had loved. *Paternity* and *test* were two words he never wanted to hear paired up again. "I only came to Texas because my mom suggested it. She thought it was time for me to make peace with my dad. And myself."

Kelly scooted her chair forward, just enough, Shane noticed, to keep her tummy from bumping the table. He had the feeling she had come to Texas to make peace with herself, too. She looked pretty today, her hair spilling out of a messy ponytail, her face void of makeup. He admired her fresh, clean glow. The aura of motherhood.

"How did you get interested in big cats?" she asked. "It's not a very common interest. Not to the degree of living with one."

He had to smile. Puma hadn't been the easiest roommate. "When I was a boy, I started having dreams about cougars. My grandma called it mountain lion medicine. She was pretty deep into the old ways. Comanches are supposed to know the difference between a regular dream and a revelation, and she said I wasn't having ordinary dreams. She convinced me that mine were special. They were my *puha* or power. And that meant they would guide me someday."

"And they did," Kelly commented. "You run a rescue now. That's pretty special."

"Thanks." He resisted the urge to cup her cheek, touched by the awe in her voice. "The mountain lion in my dreams was different than most. He only had one eye."

Her stunned gaze met his. "Oh, my God, Shane."

"Yeah, well, it wasn't as mystical as my Grandma made it sound. I thought so at first, certain that I had found this magical animal, but in actuality, Puma was just a cougar. Sure, he represented a vision, but he was still a dangerous animal. Everyone, including my dad, thought I was insane to bring him into the cabin with me. Of course no amount of reasoning was going to stop me."

"Where did Puma come from? Who had him before you?"

He sighed. "You mean who caused his eye to rupture? That's a story in itself." He could see that Kelly wanted to hear it, so he decided it was time to check on Zuni. It wouldn't do to talk about one animal while another got into trouble. He'd learned firsthand that exotics didn't behave like domestics, no matter how cute and fluffy they were.

"Just looking for Zuni," he told Kelly while he circled the room. He caught sight of the kitten and smiled. The serval wasn't interested in making mischief. She slept peacefully on a braided area rug.

Shane settled back into his seat. "The Mendozas got a call from this terminally ill man named Alex who was looking for a home for his cougar," he began. "So my dad and I went to Alex's house to check out his story. I was working actively at the rescue by this time, learning everything I could about the cats." But he had yet to heal. Tami and the baby still occupied his thoughts, and mental pictures of that family-stealing lawyer had kept the hurt and resentment alive. "Anyway, Alex's story checked out, even if he was a bit eccentric."

Shane explained that Alex had purchased Puma from an auction with the intention to raise the kitten for a while, then release him into the wild. "This can't be done, not in this manner. Once a cat imprints with people, they can't be expected to behave like an exotic who has lived in the wild. They become a danger to themselves and humans as well."

"Why?" she asked.

"They tend to venture too close to civilization, and that can lead to disaster. The animal usually ends up taking a bullet or hurting someone."

"I never thought about that."

"Most people don't. So basically that's how Puma came to me. Alex had bottle-fed him, but wasn't given proper feeding instructions, so Puma suffered from it and lost his eye. After that, Alex spared no expense to take care of the cat. He learned everything he could and realized he couldn't set Puma free. But when Puma was about four months old, Alex's disease progressed, so he started searching for someone to adopt his one-eyed cougar."

"You," Kelly said.

"Yeah, me. And I agreed to all of Alex's crazy demands. I mean, he was dying, and I had been dreaming about a one-eyed mountain lion all of my life. We were both a little mixed up. I promised him that I wouldn't cage Puma, at least not until I could afford to build the cougar a natural habitat. The rescue wasn't set up the way it is now. The compounds weren't very extravagant, and he wanted the best for his cat. He had been babying the hell out of Puma, guilty about what he'd done.''

"So you inherited a spoiled cougar."

"Yeah, but Puma was still young then, and I fooled myself into believing that living with him was going to be fairly easy. I was still a little too caught up in those dreams.''

"I'll bet you were in for a rude awakening.''

"Yeah." He grinned. "But I was too stubborn to admit it. I didn't want my dad having the last word—the 'I told you so.' I kept Puma in the cabin with me for over two years. Eventually he even shared my bed, although I wouldn't recommend it. There's nothing worse than waking up with a hundred-and-eighty-pound cat who wets the bed.''

Kelly burst into laughter. "You're crazy, Shane.''

"No, sweetheart," he teased, striking an austere pose. "I've got mountain lion medicine.''

Her expression turned suddenly serious. "You really do. And so does this cabin." She looked around, her voice respectful. "That's why I feel so close to Puma. In a way, he still lives here.''

Shane only nodded. He wished Puma had all the answers, that the cougar could tell him how to heal Kelly Baxter's heart. Ten days, he thought with an inward grimace. He had ten days to change the course of her life. He closed his eyes. Somehow that just didn't seem possible. Mountain lion medicine or not.

Rain fell from the sky the following day, muddying the ground. Parking in front of the One Stop, Kelly dashed inside the mini mart. White-haired, bearded Barry Hunt sat behind the counter.

"Afta'noon." He greeted her, speaking around his usual wad of tobacco.

Did he ever spit that stuff out? she wondered. And if he did, did it trickle onto his beard? Kelly tried not to wrinkle her nose. "Do you think you could give me directions into town?"

He shifted his behind. He wore bib-overalls, looking like a cross between a dirt-poor farmer and a grizzly old miner who'd just struck gold—in his mouth. Despite the tobacco, he grinned, displaying a shiny metal tooth. "Suppose I could. You here for some sandwich fixings?"

"Not today." Kelly had a craving for some real food—her favorite treat—cantaloupe and vanilla ice cream. Chicken sounded good, too, seasoned with curry and served with a side of steamed rice. "I thought I'd shop in town."

He grunted and poked a finger out. "Yer belly's gettin' bigger."

Gee, the man was so tactful. "Babies grow," she said, picking up a package of powdered doughnuts. She knew Barry wouldn't let her go until she bought something. "How about those directions?"

She took out a pen and a scrap of paper from her pocketbook and scribbled furiously while Barry supplied her with country instructions, things like "turn right at the Newton's place, then travel on yonder to the Harris Farm, and if you see Mrs. Harris, ask her when she's gonna bring me another jar of that elderberry jam her Aunt Millie made."

Kelly did her best to pry streets names and clearer descriptions out of Barry, paid for the doughnuts and rushed back to her utility vehicle, dodging puddles in her quest.

The windshield wipers swept across the glass. The weatherman had claimed the rain would be short-lived, although another storm would soon follow. Spring was unpredictable, Kelly thought. Clear one day, wet the next.

She angled the utility vehicle onto another narrow stretch and realized she had taken a wrong turn somewhere. The road ahead ended at a fallen tree, one that had probably blocked this path for years.

She backed the vehicle up and cursed Barry's directions. She hadn't found the Newton's blue house or the ranch that belonged to the Harris family. In fact she hadn't seen anything remotely resembling civilization.

Kelly attempted a different route, but failed. She ended up on another dirt road, one that appeared to lead to nowhere. The highway to Duarte wasn't anywhere in sight. Texas didn't look quite so appealing covered in mud. Wild grass and brush littered the ground, making landmarks nearly impossible. One acre of earth seemed as lonely as the next, the scattered hills no help at all.

Kelly tore into the doughnuts. Don't cry, she told herself, even though her eyes had begun to burn. Don't turn into a hysterical female. She drove and drove, in circles probably, spilling powdered sugar and blinking away tears.

When a familiar hilltop came into view, she squinted through the windshield. Home. Or close enough. She wiped her watery eyes. She recognized Shane and Dr. McKinley's house. The potted plants and cow skulls had never looked so inviting.

She knocked on the door. All she needed was some good solid directions. And some groceries from the supermarket, wherever that was.

Dr. McKinley answered. "Well, hello, Kelly. Come on in."

Rainwater had curled his hair, she noticed, and dampened his clothes. He padded through the house in white socks, but as they entered the kitchen, she spotted a pair of muddied boots by the back door.

"I made some rounds today," he told her. "Checked up on one of Shane's cats, too. A tiger named Sammy."

Kelly nodded. She remembered Shane had said that Sammy had a poor immune system. "I just stopped by for some directions into town."

"Oh, sure." He placed a teapot on the stove. "How about some hot chocolate first? You look a little teary-eyed, hon. Is everything okay?"

"I got lost," she admitted, realizing she had a lot more to cry about than that. She had spoken to her mother last night and learned that Jason still hadn't returned from his trip. Of course her mother had started in about the paternity suit again, spewing insults about Jason and his family. "I drove around for over an hour."

"Then some hot chocolate will help." Tom reached into the cabinet. "Little marshmallows, too."

Kelly smiled and removed her jacket. Dr. McKinley had an easy way about him. It was hard to believe that he had agreed to raise one son and not the other. But then she supposed saving his marriage had been his priority at the time. Her smile fell. She wondered if Jason would marry someday. And have other children. Sons and daughters he would welcome into his life.

They sat at the table and sipped their drinks, rain slashing against the kitchen window.

"Shane's cats don't like me much," Tom said. "They see me coming and they run into their lockdowns."

She tilted her head. "Why?"

"Because they know I'm the guy with the dart gun. Being a vet doesn't make you popular, at least not with your patients."

The image of a four-hundred-pound tiger hiding from Dr. McKinley had Kelly smiling again.

The back door blew open just then, bringing in a gust of cool air and Shane Night Wind with it. Rain dripped from the brim of his hat, and a tan duster trailed to his knees.

"Oh, this is nice, Dad," he said, winking at Kelly. "You're sitting at the table with a pretty girl, and I'm soaked to the bone."

"I was out there, too," Tom reminded his son good-naturedly. "And so was Kelly. She got lost going into town."

"It's true, I never made it," Kelly admitted as Shane wiped his boots on an indoor mat. "I drove around in circles until I ended up here. I came to the door to get directions."

"And I plied her with chocolate," Tom added, raising his cup.

"Well, you're a fine pair." Shane strode over to Kelly and

draped his coat over a rattan chair. "I'll give you a ride into town. You shouldn't be driving in this weather."

The man had an overly protective nature, she decided. But she liked him. A lot. "I'm from Ohio. It snows there."

"Yeah, well, this is Duarte, Texas. And it's been known to flood here. Storms are rare, but they do happen." He tipped his hat, spilling droplets of water onto the glass tabletop. "Besides, I can give you the grand tour."

The grand tour, Kelly learned an hour later, existed of a post office, a diner with a jukebox selection at every table, a cowboy bar called the Two Step and a run-down motel known as Duarte Flats. The market sat between a Laundromat and a pharmacy that sold cherry colas and root beer floats. The entire town faced the highway, a paved road that led to other small Texas establishments in other small Texas towns. Of course there was plenty of empty land in between.

"We've got one physician in town," Shane said, as they entered the market. "His practice is up the road. He's got a little clinic in front of his house. It's not much, but Doc Lanigan is a good old guy."

"I thought the expression was good ol' boy."

He grinned. "Yeah, that, too."

The old-fashioned market differed from the superstore where Kelly worked. There were only three check stands and no scanners. Her hometown seemed like a major metropolis compared to Duarte. Fast-food chains didn't exist in this tiny West Texas town, and she ventured to guess the privately owned market didn't offer union benefits, either.

Shane pushed the cart, and Kelly loaded it. They stood in front of the spice rack, looking for powdered curry. "Don't see any," he said.

She supposed Indonesian dishes weren't a favorite in Duarte. "How about tarragon?"

He scanned the shelf. "Nope."

She settled on a bottle of imported teriyaki sauce. As they continued up and down the aisles, her stomach jumped and jittered, making her wonder if the baby suffered from a case of hiccups. Kelly placed a calming hand over the commotion, feeling suddenly sad. She wanted to share moments like this with the father of her child. She had never planned on being a single parent.

She looked over at Shane. What would he do if he impregnated a woman he didn't love? Would he marry her? Become the husband and father Jason wasn't willing to be?

Shane turned toward her. "Steak, right?"

"What?" She realized they stood at the meat counter, the butcher waiting for her to make a selection. "No, chicken."

"This is beef country," Shane countered. "The steaks here are so fresh they practically moo."

That thought didn't hold appeal. "Chicken breasts," she told the butcher. "Fillets." She ordered enough for two hearty portions and then chose halibut for another home-cooked meal. Aside from her frantic, teary-eyed doughnut bout and an occasion bowl of ice cream, her baby had gotten used to low cholesterol foods.

"Puma likes chicken," Shane said as they moved on. "Except he takes his feathers and all."

Kelly winced. "Remind me not to invite him to dinner." She studied her neighbor's teasing smile. He was so easy to talk to, so easy to consider a friend. "What about you?"

He steered the cart toward the produce section. "I prefer my fowl without the feathers."

She laughed and bumped his arm. "I was inviting you to have dinner with me tonight."

"Oh." He grinned. "Okay. Sure."

An elderly woman walked by and smiled, but not with the kind of smile that said she knew Shane. Kelly realized the lady had mistaken them for an expectant couple—happily married and awaiting the birth of their first child. Loneliness stabbed her chest like Juliet's dagger.

She lifted a cantaloupe. Should she tell Shane about Jason? Ask for his opinion about the paternity suit? Turning the melon, she examined it without really seeing. She was leaving in nine days. She wouldn't have access to Shane's friendship forever, and she had come to Texas to make an important decision. Kelly took a deep, nervous breath. Shane had offered to listen once before.

But still…

She set the melon down and picked up another. Maybe she should warn him to be prepared for a serious dinner conversation that night.

"Are you very good at giving advice?" she asked.

"About what?" He glanced down at her hand, then back up, his amused gaze meeting hers. "Cantaloupe?" He made a show of sniffing the air. "Truthfully, I'm more of a watermelon guy myself."

Her pulse tripped. "I was thinking more along the lines of what I should do about my life."

His expression turned serious, the amber sparkle in his eyes softening to a pale glow. "I don't know if I'm much good at handing out advice, but I'll be here if you need me."

"Thank you." Kelly placed a cantaloupe in the basket, trying to appear unaffected by the gentle sound of his voice. The kindness he offered.

I'll be here if you need me.

Jason Collier, not Shane Night Wind, should have whispered those words.

She had heard that unborn babies choose their parents, that their tiny spirits decide who will give them life. Kelly cradled her tummy, comforting her womb. If her child wanted Jason for a father, then maybe, just maybe, Shane could help her find a way to make that happen.

Four

Shane walked into Kelly's cabin, dripping rain. He handed her a bouquet of mixed flowers. "For the table," he said.

The flowers were wet, she noticed, glistening with beads of water. "Thank you. Did you pick them?"

"Yeah." He reached into his coat pocket and removed a small bundle of what looked like dried herbs. "I brought some sage along, too."

She studied the offering. A fragrant aroma rose from it. "Do you want me to season the chicken with it?" she asked, feeling a bit perplexed. The chicken breasts were already in the oven, baking in a marinade of teriyaki sauce, rings of canned pineapples on top.

A smile spread across his face, softening his features. "This is for smudging. I thought it would be good for the baby."

Kelly glanced down at her tummy, then back up at her dinner guest. "Smudging?"

He stepped farther into the room. "You've never burned sage?"

Dumbfounded and still holding the flowers, she shook her head. Why would burning a dried herb be good for her baby?

Shane removed his duster and placed it on the barrel chair. His rain-dampened hair had been plaited into two long braids. Aside from pictures of Indians in history books, she had never seen a man with his hair braided. It suited him, she decided, complemented his striking features and masculine clothes.

"Your granddaddy used to smudge," he said, nodding to the cedar chest. "Isn't there a small clay pot in there? And some loose feathers?"

"I think so." There were all sorts of interesting items in the chest, Texas trinkets she assumed her grandpa had collected.

She knelt to open the trunk. Shane lowered himself to his knees beside her. He found the articles he was looking for, and she came across a mason jar for the flowers. He clasped her hand to help her up. Kelly could have sworn she'd gained at least five pounds this week.

They walked to the dining table, and she placed the bouquet between two tall, white candles. She had already set the table with Grandpa's chipped stoneware.

"Smudging is a purifying ceremony," Shane explained. "Sage, cedar or sweetgrass can be used. It rids the environment of negative energy." He lit the bundle, then fanned it with a feather.

Kelly watched as he circled the cabin and directed the smoke, cleansing each area. When he returned to the table, he lifted his gaze to hers. "I can smudge you if you'd like."

Curious, she whispered a shy "okay" and tried to picture her grandpa doing this.

Shane positioned himself in front of her, then backed up slowly, searching, he said, for the energy field that surrounded her, an aura he hoped to feel.

What would he find? she wondered nervously. Her tattered emotions? The loneliness that followed her each day?

Kelly kept her eyes trained on him, and as he came closer and fanned the fragrant smoke, she began to relax. The experience had become almost mystical. His hazy form looked like that of an ancient warrior, a vision drifting through the fog.

Shane Night Wind intrigued her. Even his name stirred an engaging image—this man who rescued cougars, picked wild-flowers in the rain, braided his hair.

They stared at each other through the sage-scented haze. "Thank you," she said. "For thinking of the baby."

He set the clay pot on the table. "You're welcome."

She wanted to take his hand and place it against her tummy. The baby was moving gently—a tiny angel fluttering its wings—cleansed and whole, awaiting the world.

"I should check on dinner," she said when the moment turned much too quiet. She couldn't possibly reach for his hand. What would he think?

They ate fifteen minutes later, seated across from each other at the scarred table, rain slashing against a small window. The sage had burned out, but the candles were lit, white wax melting, golden flames dancing.

Her nervousness returned. She had no idea how to start the conversation they both knew was supposed to take place.

Shane looked up from his plate. The ice in his glass crackled. Kelly could hear everything, including the pounding of her own heart.

"It's okay," he said. "We can talk about what's bothering you after dinner."

She startled, a forkful of food frozen in her hand. "Can you read minds? You always seem to know what I'm thinking."

The flickering candlelight illuminated his features, hollowing his cheekbones even more. "Sometimes I feel things, other people's emotions, I guess." He lifted his glass and smiled. "But I'm not psychic. I'm just observant, that's all."

Fascinated, she leaned forward. "What about earlier? Did I really have an energy field around me?"

"I think everyone does, but I can't always feel them." He caught her gaze and held it. "But with you I did."

His admission made her heart pound a little faster. "I've never met anyone like you before."

His lips tilted into another small smile. "Nor I you."

They fell silent then, a stillness that intensified the rain—a companionable quiet, Kelly thought, indoor warmth amid a spring storm. She studied him while they ate—the angular shape of his face, gold in his eyes, the mannerisms that seemed so naturally cat-like.

"Have you always worn your hair long?" she asked finally.

Shane nodded. "I was taught that a Comanche man should take pride in his hair." He set his fork down and picked up his water. "They were a bit obsessive in the old days, though. Sometimes they would attach horsehair to their own to make it longer. Or they would beg locks off a mourning woman."

"Comanche women cut their hair when someone died?"

"Sometimes the men did, too. But not as often as the women."

Kelly's mind drifted to her grandpa. Ten months had passed, but she still mourned him. She glanced at the clay pot, wondering if Shane had taught the older man the practice of smudging. Grandpa's Texas vacations seemed almost secretive now. Magical, too.

"Will you light the sage again?" she asked. She liked the earthy aroma, the calming effect of the scented smoke.

He smiled. "Sure."

While the dried herb smoldered, they cleared the table, then sat in the main room sampling Kelly's favorite dessert—cantaloupe and vanilla ice cream. Shane reclined in a leather chair, and she claimed the sofa. The rain hadn't let up; it crashed against the windows in crystalline sheets.

"My mother and I haven't been getting along lately," she said, knowing her statement wouldn't seem out of the blue to Shane. If he was sensing her emotions, then he would understand the direction she was taking.

He set his half-eaten dessert aside. "Because of the baby?"

"Because of the baby's father," Kelly admitted hastily. "She wants me to force him into taking a paternity test."

She waited for Shane to respond, but he just sat there, staring at her. She glanced down at her ice cream, wishing he would say something. Anything. Talking about this proved difficult enough, but now his strained silence managed to clog her throat.

Paternity test. Those familiar words banged against Shane's chest like a row of brass knuckles. Already he could feel welts forming on his heart, recalling bruises from his past.

He steadied his gaze and tried to focus on Kelly. She needed a friend, someone to talk to. Reliving the pain from his marriage wasn't going to do either one of them any good.

"Who is your baby's father?" he asked. And why was her mother rallying for a paternity test?

Kelly's breath hitched. "His name is Jason Collier. But he never paid much attention to me, except for a smile or two when we were in high school...."

Her words drifted, and Shane decided she was recalling the teenage smiles this Jason character had given her. "So he wasn't your high school sweetheart?"

"Heavens, no. He was one of the most popular boys at Tannery High. He dated cheerleaders and girls from prestigious families."

Shane didn't like the inflection in Kelly's voice, the tone that said she didn't think she measured up to Jason's standards. As an image of himself and Tami came to mind, he pushed it away. There had been a time when he had questioned his self-worth, too.

Kelly toyed with her ice cream. "I was shocked when Jason asked me out last summer. Of course he knew I was attracted to him, but I never expected him to act on it."

"So you dated him?"

"For two weeks before we—" She glanced away quickly.

"Slept together?" Shane provided, wondering why the admission made Kelly uncomfortable. She was twenty-four years old. Having a lover was natural.

"It was my first time," she offered suddenly.

Surprised, he leaned forward. When a glimmer of shame drifted across her face, he frowned. Virginity hadn't dawned on him. "That's okay. Everybody has to have a first time."

She placed her dessert on the coffee table. The ice cream had begun to melt, pooling inside the cantaloupe half. "It wasn't okay," she whispered. "I mean… I wasn't very good at it." She sighed and raised her voice to a more audible level. "I don't know, maybe it was nerves. Jason was going out of town for a month, and that seemed like such a long time to be without him. I was a little desperate, I suppose, not quite myself."

A knot formed in Shane's stomach. "He pressured you?"

She shook her head. "No. I was inexperienced, but I thought lovemaking would bring us closer, that when he returned he would be anxious to resume our relationship."

"And he wasn't?"

"He was angry when he found out I was pregnant."

Her eyes misted. Shane noticed they had changed colors, the deep hazel washing to a pale brown. She looked hollow, he thought, and sad, so very sad. What kind of jerk was this Jason, anyway?

"Are you in love with him?" he asked.

Those faded eyes shifted focus, away from his questioning stare. He wanted her to say no. For some unfounded reason, he didn't want her to be in love.

Shane righted his posture. Not loving a jerk would be easier on her, he told himself. The churning in his stomach wasn't jealousy, it was concern.

"I don't know, maybe," she said finally. "I think about him a lot, and thinking about him makes me ache." She twisted the napkin on her lap, then tore at it, spilling tiny pieces onto her dress. "He's very charming, or he was before I got pregnant. Jason's handsome and friendly. Both men and women like him. He was popular in high school because he was nice to people."

Shane got an image of a young entrepreneur—clean-cut,

well-spoken, well educated—just like the lawyer who had turned Tami's head.

The churning in his gut intensified. "I suppose he's rich."

Kelly practically jumped to her feet. The shredded napkin flew to the floor, the tiny pieces scattering. "I can't believe you said that."

She tore out of the room, Shane staring after her. He waited a beat before he followed her.

She had retreated to the kitchen, her back to the open doorway. He couldn't see her face, but it didn't take a genius to know she was crying. Not loud enough to hear, he realized. Soft tears spilled from her eyes, the kind that ached. Tears he had somehow caused.

"Kelly?" He moved closer and reached for her hair, but before making contact, he dropped his hand. "I'm sorry. I didn't mean to upset you."

She turned slowly, her watery eyes meeting his. "You think I'm after Jason's money."

"No, I don't." She was so fragile, he thought. Her dress flowed to her ankles, a pale floral print draping elegantly over the fullness she carried. "I think you're too sweet for something like that."

She swiped at her tears as though suddenly embarrassed by them. "Jason thinks I'm after his money. When he first found out about the baby, he said it wasn't his. And then later, he accused me of getting pregnant on purpose. I'm not sure what he believes now."

Shane wanted to tell her that Jason Collier was an idiot and she should just forget about him, but he knew that advice stemmed from the clench in his gut—the reminder of his own past. Kelly cared about her baby's father, maybe even loved him. "Jason is probably just nervous. Fatherhood scares some guys."

"So you think he'll come around?" she asked, her voice still a little broken.

Shane nodded. "Yeah, I do."

"You're not just saying that to make me feel better?"

He wanted to touch her, run his fingers through her hair, graze her cheek. Consoling gestures, he told himself. He understood pain.

"I'm speaking from experience, Kelly. I told you about how guilty my dad had been over me." And Tami's lawyer factored into his opinion, too. Reluctant fathers often redeemed themselves, accepting financial and emotional responsibility for their children. After all, Kelly hadn't described Jason as a monster. A bit of a jerk, but plenty of guys overreacted to unexpected pregnancies. Not all of them turned out to be deadbeat dads.

Kelly dried the rest of her tears. "Tom didn't question your paternity, did he?"

"No." He gave in to his urge and reached for her hand, held it lightly in his. "At least not that I was told. But it's tough for a guy to know if a child is really his. Sometimes women lie. Or sometimes they just don't know for sure. Multiple lovers aren't that uncommon."

Kelly squared her shoulders, but didn't release his hand. "Jason is the only man I've been with. I didn't lie, and I'm not interested in his money. I want him to care about this baby."

"I understand." It was difficult not to raise their joined hands to his lips and brush his mouth over her knuckles, kiss the hurt away. "Come on, let's go sit down."

He led her to the front room and sat beside her on the couch. She took back her hand and placed it against her stomach. Comforting the baby, he thought.

Shane fixed his gaze on her tummy and pictured the tiny life residing there, nesting snugly amid the feminine warmth. "Babies suck their thumbs in the womb," he said before he could think to stop himself.

Kelly gave him a startled glance. "How do you know that?"

Because he had watched Evan's ultrasound video with an expectant father's pride, marveling at the wonder of life. He shrugged, hating himself for the lie. "Read it somewhere, I guess."

"Me, too," she commented. "I've read every baby book imaginable. I even brought some of them with me."

He swallowed, envying what Jason had. "You're going to be a terrific mom."

"Thank you." The break in her voice hadn't quite mended. "That means a lot to me."

The rain had stopped. Stillness engulfed the cabin. He inhaled the scent from the smoldering sage. "I think you should consider a court-ordered paternity test. Jason probably won't come around until he knows for sure that the baby is his."

"But I don't want to sue him," she countered. "It's not money I'm after, it's love and acceptance I want. Dragging Jason into court won't give my baby emotional security. And it won't make things any easier on me, either. I hate that there are people in my hometown who believe that I got pregnant on purpose."

"Why does Jason think that?"

"He..." She exhaled a heavy breath. "When he discovered that he was out of condoms, he asked me if I was 'safe.' I thought he meant from disease, but that was his way of asking if I was on the Pill. I told him yes because I misunderstood." A rosy hue flooded her cheeks. "I thought he would...you know...before he..."

"I understand what you mean," Shane supplied since she was stumbling over the words. She had expected Jason to withdraw before he climaxed.

"I know that isn't a proper birth control method," she said, her tone not quite as shy as before. "And I probably sound like some sort of imbecile for not insisting that Jason use a condom. But in spite of our misunderstanding, we're both still responsible for this baby."

Shane agreed wholeheartedly, but apparently the father in question didn't. "You're not an imbecile."

Kelly brushed a lock of hair from her eye. "At least it

happened in the dark. That made it a little easier to hide my nervousness. I don't think he knew it was my first time.''

Shane tilted his head to study her, deciding Jason hadn't treated her the way a lover should. The guy must have been too caught up in his own pleasure to give Kelly the care she deserved. Shane wouldn't have made love to her in the dark. He would have left a low light burning. And he would have catered to her needs, touched and kissed and—

"Shane?''

He blinked. Twice, maybe three times. He couldn't be sure. "Yeah?''

"So you really think I should consider a court-ordered paternity test?''

As guilt clawed its way into his mind, Shane ducked his head. He was supposed to be giving Kelly advice, not envisioning himself in bed with her, making a baby who belonged to someone else. "I'm not saying to sue Jason, just file a petition for the tests that will prove he fathered your child. He can't ignore you once he knows the truth.''

"I hope he returns to Ohio before I have the baby. Not much can get accomplished until he comes back.''

"Where is he?'' Shane asked, upset that Jason was avoiding her to such a degree. Somebody needed to pound some sense into the guy and, at the moment, Shane wished it could be him.

"I don't know. On a business trip somewhere. His family owns a string of restaurants. He travels often, but I doubt he's ever been gone this long before.''

Shane glanced down at Kelly's hands. She wore no jewelry, no bracelets or rings. No shining 14 karat gold bands or diamond promises.

If Jason had reacted more honorably, would Kelly have accepted a marriage proposal from him? Of course she would have, he decided. Kelly might be independent, but she wasn't like Shane's mother—a woman who didn't believe in marriage for the sake of a child.

Shane loved his mom, but her free-spirited ways hadn't

rubbed off on him. He valued commitment, especially for those raising children. Jason should have offered to marry Kelly. Maybe he still would. After the baby was born, the paternity test could change everything. Shane assumed Jason came from one of those rich, traditional, tight-knit families, which meant Kelly's baby would have society grandparents—the kind who found illegitimacy unacceptable. Surely they would encourage a wedding once they knew the truth.

Now why didn't that thought give him comfort?

"Eventually he might ask you to marry him," Shane said, forcing himself to accept the idea. Kelly deserved a marriage proposal, and she was already half in love with Jason.

She met his gaze with a disbelieving look. "Somehow I doubt that."

"It's possible. His family might encourage him to consider it."

She sighed. "That's what I had hoped for in the beginning. And then I started wishing for smaller things. Concerned phone calls, a ride to the doctor's office. Just the slightest indication that he cared."

"Don't worry. Your baby will have a father. I'm certain of it."

She smiled. "Is that one of your official nonpsychic feelings?"

"Yep." He grinned back at her, then stood and rolled his shoulders. "I should get going. It's late."

She came to her feet a little awkwardly, the way pregnant women sometimes did, clutching furniture for support. Shane noticed she appeared to be carrying the baby a tad lower. He searched his memories for the old wives' tale that accompanied that position. Girls were high in front, boys carried low through the hips. Or was it the other way around?

"Thank you," she said. "I really needed someone to talk to."

"No problem."

She walked him to the door. He turned to say goodbye and as he did, she leaned forward.

The hug was automatic. Gentle and right. She put her head on his shoulder and closed her eyes. He stroked her hair and felt her breath stir against his neck.

"I'm glad you're my friend," she whispered.

He swallowed around the lump in his throat. "Me, too. Promise that when you go back to Ohio, you'll keep in touch?"

She lifted her head. "I'll call every week."

"Good." He drew her closer and held tight. On this rain-soaked Texas night Kelly Baxter was right where she belonged. In the willing arms of a friend.

Five

Although the prediction of another storm brewed, the rain had stopped, giving way to a pale-blue sky and thriving greenery. Kelly sat on a log stump near the side of Puma's containment, watching the cougar with an appreciative eye and an emotional heart. Concentrating on the cat soothed her tremulous spirit. At the cabin, she had spent the morning detailing her drawings, pulling strength from the creative force. For the first time in her life, her artwork came alive, giving her a deeper sense of self-worth.

Normally she thought of herself as average, but today she felt special. Today she absorbed the elements—the rain-soaked ground, the leaves glistening on the trees, the breeze blowing by. The one-eyed cougar. The half-Comanche man.

Yes, they were part of her, too. Puma was her inspiration and Shane her friend. On this windy afternoon, Kelly wasn't a simple girl from Ohio. Complexity pumped through her veins, giving her the power to face Jason as an equal.

She had already called her attorney about the paternity tests.

Jason was her baby's father, and if it took DNA samples to prove it to him, then so be it.

Kelly smoothed her breeze-ravaged hair. Did she love Jason Collier? She honestly didn't know. Time, she decided, would tell, especially now that she had discovered a slice of inner peace. When she returned to Ohio, she would hold her head high—explore herself and her feelings.

Don't worry. Your baby will have a father. I'm certain of it.

Those words, Shane's words, soothed her like a balm. Loving Jason or hurting from his criticism wasn't the issue. Encouraging him to take an active part in his child's life was key. Kelly's father had died many years before, but thanks to her grandpa she hadn't been forced to survive without paternal love. And if she could find a way to make it happen, her baby would know paternal love, too. Once the child was born and the tests proven, how could Jason ignore the truth?

He couldn't. Shane had said that as well.

The sound of footsteps caught her attention. A smile lit her face before she turned. She knew who it was.

"Hi." Shane returned her smile, his unbound hair lifting like dark, auburn-tipped wings. "My dad told me you were out here."

"I wanted to visit with Puma. I hope you don't mind."

"Of course not. I would have rather been here than cooped up in my office. The toughest part about running a rescue is organizing fund-raisers. I'm not very social, so planning these things are a nuisance."

She glanced over at Puma. The cat, peering through a crop of vegetation, observed them through that lone eye. "A necessary one, right?" Jungle Hill had plenty of feline mouths to feed.

"Yep. A necessary nuisance. It costs about $200 a month to feed each animal," he offered, supplying an answer to the question she had yet to pose.

He shifted his stance, sporting his usual attire—a soft cotton shirt tucked into the waistband of faded jeans. Shane often wore Western hats and boots, but he didn't resemble a crisp, Texas cowboy. His gait was more fluid, that of man who had lived his life among big cats, becoming one in the process. How else could he have shared the cabin with Puma? The cougar must have thought Shane was another mountain lion.

Kelly smiled and patted her belly. Puma probably thought she was a walking watermelon.

"I like this weather," he said, stretching his arms. "If feels good to be outside."

"Yes, is does."

Kelly scooted over, leaving him a portion of the stump. He sat beside her, aware of her silent invitation. Another small wind kicked up, blowing Kelly's hair across her cheek.

"It's like wheat growing wild," he said.

She knew he meant her hair. A compliment, she decided, unpretentious poetry in Shane's quiet drawl. Strange, but a few moments ago, she had been thinking metaphorically about *his* hair.

They fascinated each other, she realized. Mutual admiration. Male and female friends.

He leaned against her shoulder. "Why do you look so different today? So free?"

"Because I know everything is going to be all right," Kelly answered. "I called my attorney this morning. I decided to follow through on the paternity test."

"Good. I'm glad."

He caught a strand of her hair and held it. Suddenly their faces were only inches apart, close enough to inhale the same gust of air—and quite possibly the flavor of each other with it. Kelly could almost taste the peppermint candy in Shane's mouth.

"What about your mom?" he asked.

"What about her?" She tried not to focus on his lips, but he kept darting his tongue over them.

"Did you talk to her? Tell her what you decided?"

"Yes." Because Kelly wanted to kiss him, she froze. A pregnant woman shouldn't want a man who wasn't responsible for her condition. She studied the shape of his lips, the moisture his tongue had made. Why hadn't her baby kicked? Wasn't it time for a scolding?

Shane blinked. His eyes looked glazed, the flecks of gold a metallic sunburst. "What were we talking about?"

Using his sturdy shoulder for support, Kelly rose to her feet, wishing the baby would give her a healthy jab of reality. Since when did she look into a man's eyes and see the sun? "My mom, I think."

"Oh, yeah." He pulled a hand through his hair, settling the metaphoric wings. "Is she okay with your decision?"

"She would prefer I file a lawsuit. Make Jason pay, so to speak. But you know how I feel about that." Yes, he knew. Shane, her dear friend with the moist, sexy lips understood better than anyone. Forcing Jason into child support and court-ordered custody visits didn't work for her. "I'm glad we're so open with each other," she added, looking directly at Shane. "I don't know what I would do without you."

"You'd do just fine."

He turned his head, and for an instant Kelly wondered if he concealed his expression. Through the mass of hair that blew around his face, she thought she detected a frown—an uneasy slant to those sensuous lips.

The following day Shane invited Kelly to go for a drive with him. He had to. It was time to open up, become the kind of friend she assumed he already was—the kind who didn't keep secrets.

I'm glad we're so open with each other.

Her words chipped at his conscience like an imaginary pickax, making the headache he'd suffered through the night quite real.

Kelly pulled the seat belt across her body. She got prettier each day—a beauty that bloomed from the inside out. The type, in Shane's opinion, that mattered most.

He turned the key and gunned the engine. "It's supposed

to start raining again tomorrow. Figured we should take advantage of the dry spell while we have the chance.''

''I packed some sandwiches.'' She motioned to a plastic grocery bag she had brought along.

''That's fine.'' He wasn't the least bit hungry. His stomach was already full—with anxiety. A cheating wife served as an appetite suppressant, even five years after the fact.

They drove in silence. He chose scenic roads for Kelly's benefit, passing cattle ranches and horse farms. She peered out the window, clearly enthralled with the grazing animals. When she *oohed* and *aahed* over a herd of mares with their foals, he couldn't help but smile.

''Sweet,'' he said, reaching over to touch her hair. She wore it loose, one side clipped away from her face with a butterfly-shaped barrette. How appropriate, he thought, studying the colorful ornament. Delicate, elusive Kelly. She would be gone in less than a week.

''I know. Aren't they adorable?'' she responded as he drove forward, her gaze still fixed on the horses.

He withdrew his hand. She hadn't realized that his ''sweet'' had been meant for her.

The next ten miles led to narrower dirt roads, distant hills and scattered brush. Kelly shifted beside him. ''It's hard to believe it's going to rain again. It's so peaceful now. Barely even a breeze.''

He pulled the four-wheel-drive off the road and parked near a gnarled old tree. ''The calm before the storm, as they say.''

Shane studied his hands while Kelly turned his way. Suddenly the truck seemed stuffy. He could barely breathe.

''Do you want to sit outside for a while?'' he asked ''I can pad the tailgate with a blanket.''

''Okay.''

She brought the lunch sack, and he folded the blanket. When she handed him a small bottle of mountain springwater, he accepted it gratefully. Not only was his breath clogged, but his mouth had gone dry.

He twisted the cap and raised the plastic to his lips, then

guzzled the cool liquid. Afterward, he helped Kelly onto the cushioned tailgate.

Silent, they sat side by side. She looked his way, but rather than turn, he stared straight ahead. He hated talking about the past, thinking about it. Reliving it through words and painful memories.

Kelly touched his shoulder. "What's wrong, Shane? You're not acting like yourself. You seem a little uneasy. I noticed it yesterday, too."

Not himself. It struck him an odd thing for her to say, even if it was true. They had known each other for such a short time, yet she had determined his mood. "Maybe this is just one side of me you've never seen," he responded in a tight voice.

She removed her hand from his shoulder. "Are you mad at me? Did I do something to upset you?"

"No, of course not." Feeling like a first-rate heel, he met her wounded gaze. "What's on my mind happened years ago." He brushed her cheek with the back of his hand, offering a physical apology. "But it's something I should have told you about before now. I haven't always been a bachelor. I was married once, and I had a child, too."

Stunned by Shane's words, Kelly looked into his eyes and noticed the absence of gold. They were dark, as lonely as the impending storm.

He'd spoken in past tense. Why would someone talk about their family in past tense? "Dear, God," she whispered. "You lost them."

"Yes, but not in the way you think." He pulled a hand through his hair. "They didn't die. It wasn't like that. It was a different kind of loss."

One he still struggled to overcome, she realized. "Do you want to talk about it?"

"No." He gave her a sad smile. "But I'm going to, anyway. I owe you this, Kelly. As a friend you have the right to know."

Suddenly his despair seemed connected to her somehow. The thought made her uneasy, but she kept the discomfort to herself. Shane seemed anxiety-ridden enough for both of them. "I'm listening."

"I met Tami in high school. Like you and Jason."

Kelly toyed with her water bottle. The parallel had already begun. "What's she like?"

"Different than me. She comes from more of everything—money, education, ambition. Her family is successful and sort of...uppity, I guess."

Like Jason's family. Kelly nodded. "I understand."

"They didn't like me much," Shane admitted. "But I pursued her anyway. And I think she was attracted to me at first because it was exciting to defy her family. I was a novelty, I suppose. The illegitimate mixed-blood who'd been raised by a free-spirited mother and an overly traditional grandmother."

"What does Tami look like?" she asked. It was a woman's question, but she couldn't help it. Was Tami Comanche or white? Tall or petite? Lean or curvaceous? What sort of girl had Shane Night Wind fallen in love with?

"I haven't seen her in years, but I suppose she looks much the same. Willowy. Long black hair, long legs, dark eyes."

Willowy. Jealousy nipped like a snapping turtle. Even the word in itself was beautiful. "She's Comanche, then?" The descendent of an Indian princess, no doubt.

"Yeah. I wouldn't have thought to date outside of my race at that time. I still hated my dad and everything I believed the white world represented." He looked down at his hands, then back up, his eyes still a distant shade of brown. "Tami was the love of my life, my best friend. The person I wanted to spend forever with."

"Did she feel that way about you, Shane?"

He shrugged, but not indifferently. The gesture hunched his shoulders, pulling him toward the center of his pain. "I thought she did, but after we got married, I guess the novelty wore off. She went to college, then got a job as a paralegal in this fancy law office, and I was just a high school graduate doing construction work. A disappointment."

Kelly wanted to console him, draw his head to her breast

and encourage him to forget. But there was more to be said, she realized, much more.

She gentled her tone, keeping her voice quiet. "Tell me the rest."

"Three years after we were married, Tami found out she was pregnant. I thought it was the best thing that could have happened to us. I was so sure the baby would make us a true family."

When Shane took Kelly's hand, she knew his pain had come full circle. His grip was shaky, almost desperate. This was how she fit into his past. Something had gone wrong while his wife was pregnant. "This is the difficult part, isn't it?"

"The beginning of it, yeah." He expelled a rough breath. "We went on with our lives, preparing for the baby—discussing names, decorating the nursery. But toward the end of her pregnancy, Tami broke down and told me the baby might not be mine. She'd had an affair with this out-of-town attorney. Some hotshot white guy, and she didn't know which one of us was the father."

Kelly kept his hand in hers. How could Tami have been with someone else when she had Shane? How could she have destroyed a beautiful young man? Saddled him with despair?

"I can't even describe how I felt," Shane went on. "When I wasn't envisioning Tami in bed with her lover, I was fighting the notion that the baby in her womb might be his." He tightened his fingers around Kelly's. "It wasn't right. I'd been a part of everything—the morning sickness, the doctor visits, the ultrasound." He glanced down at Kelly's tummy. "I felt the baby move for the first time. And I bought all those soft, fluffy toys and assembled the crib. I was the father, not him."

A soul-piercing image came to Kelly's mind. Shane alone in the newly decorated nursery, an animated mobile turning above an empty crib. His head in his hands, his heart hovering over the infant's bed. "You forgave Tami, didn't you?"

"I had to," he answered. "Her affair was over, and we were bringing a child into the world."

He was so honorable, she thought. A valiant husband, a dedicated father.

Shane met her gaze, looking as though he'd just read her mind. "It wasn't easy, not any of it. We spent the next few months in counseling trying to repair the damage. I told Tami that she had to think of the baby as mine. I made her promise that she would never ask me to take a paternity test to determine otherwise, and that she would never contact the other man for any reason."

Kelly remained quiet, giving her companion time to rein his emotions. She could see them in his eyes—those alluring, cat-like eyes.

"We had a boy," he said finally. "Evan Tyler. The perfect little *ona*."

She tilted her head. *"Ona?"*

"Baby," he clarified. "The perfect little Comanche. God, I loved him. I used to go into his room and just stare at him for hours. Watch his chest rise and fall, listen to him breathe. He had Tami's eyes, dark and kind of almond shaped, and he had my—" Shane paused, his voice turning distant and sad. "I thought he had my hair, the color and the texture, but…"

He released Kelly's hand and clenched his fist, a tightness that matched his voice. "When Evan was six months old, Tami heard from her old lover. He was opening a practice in our hometown and wanted to see her again."

"She went to him, didn't she?"

"Yes."

"What about Evan?"

"The baby turned out to be his."

A small breeze, the first stirring of wind, rustled leaves on a nearby tree. The branches reached out like arms, drooping, clawing their way to the earth. To Kelly, the image seemed fitting. Someone had stolen what belonged to Shane, torn and clawed and ripped at his heart.

"You took a paternity test?" she asked quietly.

"Yes," he answered again.

He had taken it, but not without defiance, she realized. He

had struggled to keep his son. And probably his wife, too.
"Are they together now?"

He nodded. "Tami divorced me and married him." He
gazed up at the tree, at its haunting branches. "I lost everything. Even visitation rights. I haven't seen Evan in over five
years. They told me I had no place in his life."

Kelly closed her eyes. Battling a successful attorney for custody of a child who wasn't biologically his must have been a
nightmarish ordeal. "I'm sorry," she whispered. "So sorry."

"I am, too."

As another small breeze brushed by, she felt him watching
her. She opened her eyes and saw a glint of gold in his. Just
a glint.

Unable to stop herself, she touched his face—the strong,
smooth jaw, the high ridge of his cheekbones, the lashes that
framed those exotic eyes. When she slid her fingers into his
hair, he moved even closer, just a heartbeat away.

His lips touched hers, lightly, ever so lightly. She wanted
to taste him, give and take comfort, wrap herself in his
warmth. She followed the length of his hair, encouraging the
strands to flow through her fingers.

She opened her mouth under his and felt herself slipping,
drifting on a wave. The tips of their tongues met, a solace they
both needed.

He pulled back to look at her, and when their eyes connected, he smiled.

"Motherhood is beautiful," he said, his voice a husky whisper. "You're beautiful."

A response didn't seem necessary, not now, not while he
lowered his head to nuzzle her neck. He could have been a
cat—a strong, sensual creature—sleek and lean with a hint of
auburn running through his hair and flecks of gold shining in
his eyes. He was beautiful, too. This man who had lost the
child he'd loved.

Kelly brought his hand to her tummy and felt the baby stir
in welcome. Before she went home, she wanted to share her
child with him, if only for a few brief moments.

Shane lifted his head. "I'm going to miss you."

"I know. Me, too."

She placed her hands on his shoulders, and while he splayed his fingers over her stomach, she renewed their kiss. A kiss caught between friendship and sensuality—an emotion neither would allow themselves to analyze. She would be gone soon, and then it wouldn't matter.

Three days later Shane accepted a steaming mug of tea from Kelly. She didn't drink coffee, but she kept plenty of decaffeinated tea on hand, he noticed.

Averting his gaze, Kelly sipped from her mug. "Have a seat, Shane."

He backed into the barrel chair, feeling like a nuisance. Since the storm had blown in, he stopped by the cabin daily, mooching tea and dripping water all over her hardwood floors.

"Are you sure you don't want to stay with my dad and me?" he asked. "I hate the idea of you being out here all by yourself in this weather. The roads are a mess. They never really got the chance to dry out from last time."

"Thank you, but I'll be fine," she responded. "I don't plan on going anywhere. I have plenty of reading material, and the fridge is stocked."

Shane shifted his feet. He wished he had access to Zuni to use as a bribe, but the serval kitten had gone home to her rightful owner. He couldn't very well claim that Zuni needed her, so he tried another tactic. "Is your heater working okay?"

She sat on the edge of the sofa, wearing one of her floral maternity dresses. This one bore a hint of lace. "Yes. The propane tank is full. The realtor took care of it, remember?"

"Oh, yeah." They still hadn't made eye contact, at least not for an extended period of time. It was that kiss, he decided, that had them both feeling so damn awkward. He turned toward the window. The shutters were open, exposing the rain. Pellets hit the glass like hail. "It's really coming down hard."

She followed the line of his sight. "Hasn't let up for days."

Shane nodded. It had been days since he'd touched her lips,

too. Three long, lonely days. He wondered what she would do if he initiated another kiss. One, moist flavorful taste.

He tried to catch Kelly's gaze, but noticed she appeared absorbed with the rain. Maybe kissing again wasn't such a good idea. Their friendship seemed to be suffering because of it. They had confided in each other, revealed their deepest pain, and now they couldn't get past the weather.

"What sort of stuff do you have to read?" he asked, hoping to resume a semblance of comfort between them. He didn't want to leave just yet. He wanted to be near her a while longer. She was going home on Friday, leaving his tiny corner of the world.

Kelly set her tea on a nearby table and picked up a paperback. "Suspense."

Shane felt like an idiot. If the novel had been any more obvious, he would have been the one reading it.

"I have those baby-care books, too," she added.

As he recalled the fullness of her tummy beneath his hands, his heartbeat skipped. "How is the little *ona?*"

A smile drifted across her face. "Fine. Restless, actually."

"Really?" He wanted permission to touch her again, encouragement like she'd given him on the day they'd kissed. He wanted to feel the baby move, feel it greet him with a hearty kick.

But she didn't offer, so he didn't ask. He sat in the barrel chair, still wearing his coat, his tea losing warmth, their gazes never quite meeting.

A clock could have ticked between them—one of those tall, antique timepieces that reminded people how quiet their home was. Or how uncomfortable their guest was making them.

Shane gave in to his urge to stare, study her carefully in the silence. Suddenly concerned, he scooted to the edge of his chair. Pale shadows worried her eyes, a lavender hue that made her appear frailer than usual. Even her freckles had faded a little, her cheeks lacking their usual glow. "Are you feeling all right?"

She tucked a loose stand of hair behind her ear. Most of it

had been secured with a metal clip, but a few flyaway pieces rebelled from the confinement. "Truthfully, I am a bit tired."

He knew he'd overstayed his welcome. Kelly needed her rest. He supposed the pregnancy took its toll, not to mention her personal concerns. Jason still hadn't returned to Ohio. No response had been made regarding her request for a paternity test. But court procedures didn't happen overnight, and there was still time. A test couldn't be conducted until the baby was born.

He rose to his feet. "I better get going. Promise you'll rest, okay?"

"I will." The proper hostess, she relieved him of the luke-warm tea and set the sturdy mug beside hers. "Let me walk you out."

She opened the door, and together they stepped onto the porch. A powerful wind blew the driving rain toward them, just close enough to feel the damp chill.

Her driveway was already packed with mud, the landscape pooling with water. "Another day like this and the roads might flood," he said in a last-ditch attempt to convince her to come home with him.

"I don't plan on traveling," she responded. "Besides I'm from Ohio, remember? I'm used to all sorts of weather. I'll be fine." She brushed his shoulder. "You worry too much."

"I suppose." He brought his hand to her cheek. "I'll call you tomorrow."

Her eyelids fluttered, a reaction, he thought, to his touch. A reminder of their kiss and how good it had felt. They stood a little awkwardly then. He wanted to hug her, but drew back instead.

"Go inside before you catch cold," he told her.

"Okay." She nodded and turned. "Bye, Shane."

"Bye." He stood watching her, wishing her fragility didn't make him ache. Despite her brave front, Kelly looked lost. A delicate young woman in need of protection.

Six

Kelly closed the door behind her. She was beyond tired. Exhaustion weighted her weary bones. She headed for the bedroom and opened the dresser, searching for a nightgown. She would shower, then sleep off her fatigue.

Facing Shane these past few days hadn't been easy. Whenever she saw him, she wanted to snuggle in his arms. Absorb his strength. Kiss him again. And it was wrong, she thought, to want those things. Wrong to prey on Shane's emotions. Two weeks in Texas hadn't given her the right to need him. Not when she carried Jason's child.

"I'm sorry, Shane," she said aloud, "for confusing your life. For making you think about Evan. For making you miss him all over again."

Regardless of the storm, she couldn't possibly stay at his house. Shane had given her enough of himself. And what had she given him?

She turned on the shower. Problems. She had given Shane her problems.

Kelly let the warm water sluice over her. Friday was three days away. She would be home in three days. And when would Jason be home? When would he return to face her? Soon, she hoped. Because once Jason acknowledged her concerns, kissing Shane would be a distant memory. He would be her long-distance friend. A phone call instead of flesh and blood, his masculine beauty unattainable.

Kelly glanced at her reflection in the foggy mirror. A lonely woman stared back at her. God help her. She missed him already.

Turning away from the mirror, she dried hastily, then slipped on her nightgown. Next she entered the dimly lit bedroom and climbed under the covers, sleep taking hold.

Hours later she awakened to use the bathroom. On her way back to bed, she squinted at the clock. 2:00 a.m. The rain hadn't let up; she could hear it pounding against the cabin.

Hugging herself, she glanced out the window. Tree branches loomed, the howling winds forcing them against the glass. Just the stuff horror movies were made of, she thought with a sudden chill. A girl alone in an isolated cabin, ghastly shapes forming outside her window.

Bounding off the bed, Kelly latched the shutters. She knew better than to let her imagination run amok. But even so, going back to sleep seemed out of the question. Maybe she should draw for a while, create new images in her mind. She could sketch another likeness of Puma, maybe—

Kelly gasped. A cramp clenched her stomach, sending her entire body into a tight ball.

Wide-eyed, she looked up at the window. A girl alone in an isolated cabin...

The shutters remained closed. There were no ghastly shapes haunting the glass, only pain, a terrible pain.

The baby.

No! She shook her head as the cramp subsided. Fear. Indigestion. Anything but the baby. It was too soon.

Climbing back into bed, she glanced at the phone on the nightstand. Without a second thought, she lifted the receiver.

Shane would be there in an instant. He would know what to do, he always—

Kelly's pounding heart lurched.

Silence.

No dial tone greeted her. The phone line was dead.

She tried again. Then again, punching buttons, tapping the receiver, willing it to work. She released a choppy breath, unshed tears burning the back of her eyes. Not a spark. Not the slightest sign of life.

She should have gone with him. She should have listened to Shane. With a shaky hand, Kelly placed the phone back on its cradle. She could go now. She could drive to his house.

Another day like this and the roads might flood.

Shane's words flew into her head like a warning. A pregnant woman alone on a washed-out road? Could she take that chance? Her rental vehicle wasn't a four-wheel-drive. What if it got stuck in the mud? Then where would she be?

Kelly remained in bed, rocking herself for comfort, the torrid sound of the rain an eerie companion. Once daylight surfaced, she would feel better. One severe cramp meant nothing in the scheme of things. A false labor pain. She gazed around the cabin, her eyes settling momentarily on the inactive phone. Her baby wasn't ready to come into the world. Not now. Not on the heels of a storm.

But as a burst of lightning flashed through the slats on the shutters, Kelly closed her eyes and prayed. Morning was a long way off.

Shane adjusted the hood on a yellow slicker, protecting his face from the downpour. His volunteers knew better than to show up at the rescue this morning, especially since he had refused their services during the last hard rain. He only had two volunteers, one, a biology major, interested in wildlife research; the other, a cat enthusiast, hoping to work as a trainer someday. Neither had gone beyond the stage of cleaning cages, but both proved themselves invaluable. But not today. On this turbulent morning, Shane would take full responsibility for the animals. The young men who volunteered their time didn't deserve to be caught up in this weather, fighting hazardous roads.

As he strode across familiar pathways, his rubber boots sank into the mud, making each step thick and cumbersome. Thank goodness the rescue sat on a hill, keeping the habitats free from water damage. The cats would take shelter if they so desired, surviving on instinct. Food, of course, was another matter. Meals had to be provided, come rain or shine.

A crack of thunder ripped through the heavens, giving Shane a start. He blew a windy breath. How in God's name was Kelly going to get to the airport on Friday? If the storm continued as predicted, the roads would be washed out by then, a gully of nothing but water. Didn't she realize how primitive Duarte was? Damn it. Shane grabbed the front of his jacket as a strong gust threatened to pull it open. Why hadn't he insisted that she stay with him?

Well, he sure as hell would today. He'd call her as soon as his work was done. And he'd demand a postponement of her trip, too. He wouldn't allow her to leave until the storm passed. This weather wasn't safe.

Shane sighed. At least it wasn't a twister, one of those run-for-the-storm-cellar tornadoes Mother Earth raged upon Texas. As long as Kelly remained indoors, she would be fine. She was probably curled up in bed with a book, sipping that berry tea she liked so well, refreshed from a much-needed sleep.

The tears burning Kelly's eyes threatened to fall. She had been willing herself not to cry, insisting her labor was false, that the intermittent pains throughout the night didn't mean the baby was coming. But now she knew different. Her water had broken.

The front of her nightgown bore a large stain, the fabric damp and clingy. She twisted the hem and held tight. How soon before the next pain arrived? How far apart had they been?

She didn't know. God help her, but she honestly didn't

know. Nor could she count how many times she had tried the phone.

Kelly lifted the receiver yet again. The silence was deafening. As she returned it to its cradle, the tears she'd struggled to contain made their way down her cheeks.

Feeling like a child who had lost her way, Kelly cried. A silent, dazed, lonesome cry. Daylight hadn't eased her fear. The shutters were open, yet gloom enveloped the cabin, rain pounding the roof like a thousand angry fists.

Her baby was coming, and she was alone, trapped in a vicious storm.

Where was Shane? Yesterday he'd said that he would call. Surely he would check on her once he discovered her phone line was dead.

How many hours would pass before he attempted to call? She clutched the damp section on her nightgown. Two? Three? By then, it might be too late.

Too late.

The thought nearly knocked the wind out of her. Catching her breath through small, shaky gasps, she studied her surroundings. An antique armoire stood in lieu of a closet, a rough-hewn dresser displayed a wrought-iron candelabra and a scarred wooden nightstand held a useless telephone. This room, this rustic old room, would be the place in which her child would enter the world. Cry its first cry. Focus its tiny eyes on its mother.

Kelly sniffed, then dabbed at her runny nose, her plan suddenly clear. No more tears. It was time to get a hold of herself and start behaving like a mother. Her baby needed her strong and whole.

Making her way to the dresser, she removed her soiled nightgown and panties. Opting for a sleeveless cotton gown, she slipped it over her head and secured the ribbon at the bodice. Aside from her trembling hands, the task proved relatively easy.

The damp sheets were another matter. She struggled with the corners of the mattress, fearing another pain would immobilize her. Unable to secure the clean linen properly into place, she tucked it haphazardly, grateful she had come this far, her rebellious limbs shaky and weak.

At least her baby would be born on fresh sheets, she told herself, using the headboard for support. As she eased herself onto the bed, she caressed the posts, wondering if she would grip them later, if the cool, dark wood would be her salvation.

Don't get melodramatic. Stay strong. Be prepared.

Forcing herself to stand once again, she gathered clean towels and stacked them on the nightstand. Beside the towels, she placed a small pair of scissors and an antiseptic in which to sterilize them. She didn't know much about delivering a child, but she knew this much—she wasn't about to gnaw her way through the umbilical cord.

The image made her laugh—a laughter she prayed her baby could feel. She didn't want the child to absorb her fear, the overwhelming panic rising in her throat.

Would she need a basin of water? Damp washcloths? A makeshift...

Kelly's questions went unanswered. The severity of her next pain pitched her forward. She collapsed onto the bed, knowing the onset of hard labor had begun.

Soaked to the bone, his boots sloshed with mud, Shane entered his house through the back door. He stood in the cluttered service porch that led to the kitchen and removed his rain slicker and boots. Normally he just wiped his feet on the kitchen mat, but then his legs weren't usually knee-deep in mud. Scanning the clothes rack for dry garments, he blessed his dad for having the good sense to do their laundry that morning. He checked his watch and frowned. Morning? It was almost noon. He'd been outside for hours.

Shrugging out of water-logged Levi's, he washed up in a utility sink, drying his face and hands on a nearby towel. After donning clean jeans and a denim shirt, he headed for the kitchen, hoping his dad had a strong pot of midday coffee brewing.

Tom was in the kitchen, but the smell of roasting beans wasn't wafting through the air.

"What's going on?" Shane asked.

His dad stood at the counter, inserting batteries into a heavy-duty flashlight. An arsenal of portable lights littered the table, including several kerosene lanterns.

"The power has been going on and off. I figure it's just a matter of time before it's gone for good," Tom said, emphasizing his statement by motioning to the microwave clock where bright red zeros flashed across the display panel.

Shane raked his hands through his rain-dampened hair. The day had gone from bad to worse, and it was barely noon. "I better call Kelly."

The older man tested the flashlight, shining the beacon across the room. "I don't understand why she didn't come home with you yesterday."

"Tell me about it. I guess I should have insisted." He reached for the phone. "But you know how stubborn women can—" The disconnected line rammed him like a hard punch to the gut. He gulped the air that whooshed out.

Something was wrong. Terribly wrong. Why hadn't he sensed it before now?

"Dad," he said, his voice catching on the lump in his throat. "Will you come with me to Kelly's place? I think she's going to need us."

The kitchen light flickered, then went out altogether, but neither man paid it any mind. "Why? What happened? Didn't she answer?"

"The phone's dead."

Tom's ruddy features relaxed. "That's no reason to panic, Shane."

"But I've got this awful feeling." A feeling he couldn't shake, a sudden ache in the pit of his stomach. "Besides, Kelly didn't seem well yesterday. She was overly tired. And she looked so pale."

Further explanation wasn't necessary. Tom accepted his son's response, and together they worked side by side, hastily gathering emergency supplies. The power appeared to be off for good, and the possibility that Kelly was ill plagued them both. Once they reached the cabin, they would probably remain there, at least for the night.

"Get some blankets," Tom said, as he headed outside to load Shane's truck.

Shane tore off down the hall. Thank God for his father's organizational skills. It was Tom who kept hurricane supplies in the cellar—bottled water, non-perishable foods and over-the-counter medicine that would come in handy in case Kelly was sick. There were probably blankets in the cellar, too, but Shane raided the linen closet instead. He was too damn nervous to think straight.

He tossed the blankets into the extra cab of the truck, then glanced at his watch. They had packed within a matter of minutes.

The road conditions were bad, but not as troublesome as Shane had feared. The tires spun through a sludge of mud at the bottom of the hill, but the four-wheeler made it through without incident. A smaller vehicle might not have fared so well. He exhaled an anxious breath, grateful the Ford hadn't let him down.

Shane turned onto the narrow road that led to the cabin, then exchanged a nervous glance with his father. Debris floated in pools of water, tree branches and leaves that had fallen by the wayside. He maneuvered the truck toward their final destination, his heart pounding faster than the rain.

The cabin looked more isolated than usual, a tiny wooden structure surrounded by vast amounts of foliage and a weather-beaten porch. Shane prayed Kelly was safe and warm inside, that the knot in his gut wasn't what it seemed.

He thumped his fist against the door, hoping to be heard above the storm. His father stood beside him, tall and quiet. Shane knew Tom took his premonitions seriously, which, at the moment, wasn't a comforting thought. Shane wanted to be wrong this time.

"Damn it, why isn't she answering?" He pounded again, then yelled through the door. "Kelly! It's me! Shane!"

When she didn't appear, he turned to his dad. "What should we do?"

Just as Tom began to form an answer, the door opened. Shane could see the change of expression on his father's face. He turned back and caught sight of Kelly.

Sweat bathed her skin, and her wheat-colored hair hung in limp strands. Pale, he thought. Deathly pale. As he opened his arms, she stumbled into them and burrowed against his chest.

"The baby's coming," she said, her voice barely audible. "Soon."

"It's okay, sweetheart, we're here now." Shane lifted her off the ground, then realized he had just violated an ancient taboo—Comanche men, other than medicine men, were not permitted to be present during childbirth, let alone participate in labor.

A balloon of panic burst in his chest, but he continued to hold her, praying silently for forgiveness.

He entered the cabin, Tom on his heels. Whether his father had heard Kelly's words or understood by instinct, Shane couldn't be sure. Either way, Tom seemed to know exactly what was happening.

The older man took charge. As Shane settled Kelly onto the bed, Tom held her hand and asked about her labor, his tone gentle and soothing. She answered in a quiet, shaky voice, tears glazing her eyes. Tears of relief, tears of discomfort. Shane thought her expression mirrored conflicting emotions.

"I deliver babies all the time," Tom told her. "You're going to be fine."

Shane knew the babies the veterinarian delivered were gangly foals and spotted calves, but that didn't seem to matter. Tom McKinley was a doctor just the same—a medicine man.

While Tom scrubbed his hands, Shane sat beside Kelly, confused and fearful. He reached out to stroke her hair, then drew back. He couldn't continue to touch her. Not now.

Grandma had instilled the old ways into him, and she had

been so strong in her convictions, Shane had respected her wishes by keeping his distance during Evan's birth. Rather than remain by Tami's side, he had behaved like a nineteenth-century father, waiting quietly for the announcement.

Tom returned from the bathroom and gave Shane a verbal list of articles to gather. He did as his father bade and noticed some of the items were already on the dresser. His heart clenched. Sweet little Kelly had been preparing to deliver her own child. God help him, but how could he walk away now? How could he explain that he had no right to be there?

Thirty minutes might have passed. Or possibly an hour. Shane had no idea, although he assumed his dad knew. Tom appeared to be timing the contractions, cramping pains that rammed through Kelly with the force of a Mack truck. Each time they hit, she pitched forward and bit back a scream, her lips straining from the pressure.

Protect her. Please, keep her safe.

His hands clasped tightly in his lap, Shane prayed once again—prayed that his now deceased grandmother was mistaken, that his masculine presence wouldn't harm Kelly or her baby.

Tom remained at the foot of the bed. He had draped Kelly's lower half with a sheet, for modesty's sake, Shane assumed. The sheet tented around her drawn knees.

"It's not time to push," Tom told her. "Not just yet."

Kelly gazed up at Shane when the pain subsided. He still sat beside her, silent and nervous, clutching a portion of the sheet to keep himself from touching her. He struggled between the old ways and the new—never quite knowing where he fit in. He wanted to touch her, wanted to give her a part of himself, yet he had been taught...

She touched him instead, her shaky hand connecting with his.

"Hold me," she whispered. "Please."

Unable to deny her plea, he reached forward. She felt as fragile and frightened as she looked. Her lips were parched, her skin bathed in sweat, her heartbeat erratic. It pounded

against her rib cage—hard and fast, just like his own. He
stroked her matted hair, offering strength and comfort. It felt
right, he thought, to take her in his arms—to keep her there.

When Kelly's next contraction hit, Tom ordered her to push,
and she did so willingly. Shane supported her shoulders, holding her as close as humanly possible. Over and over she
pushed, clinging to him as though he provided a lifeline.

Grandma had been wrong. Kelly needed him. He couldn't
possibly harm her. Nor could he endanger her child.

On the wings of Shane's revelation came a strong infant
cry. His breath hitched until Tom's proud voice seized the
moment.

"It's a girl," the doctor said, placing the tiny babe against
her mother. "And she's perfect."

The next hour was the most incredible sixty minutes of
Shane's life. Not only had he participated in Kelly's labor, but
he had helped his father prepare the baby for her introduction
into the world. With Tom's instruction, Shane had bathed the
golden-haired infant, then brought her back to Kelly swaddled
in a downsized blanket.

As he lowered the baby into Kelly's arms, their eyes met—
just long enough to make his breath catch. As he stepped back,
Kelly unwrapped her daughter, then inspected tiny fingers and
toes, counting each one, cooing as she did.

Shane smiled. He had done that, too. He had examined
every tiny appendage while marveling at the baby's perfection.

Tom sat beside Kelly as Shane stood back, absorbing the
moment.

"Thank you," Kelly said to the doctor, "for everything."
She looked weary, yet beautiful, an elated new mother, tired
eyes shining.

The older man touched the newborn's cheek. "Have you
thought of a name?"

Kelly nodded. "Brianna Lynn."

"Brianna Lynn." Tom tested the sound on his tongue, his
Texas twang taking on a lilting brogue, something Shane had

never heard his father do. "'Tis a fine Irish name for a wee Irish lass. Your grandpa would be proud."

Kelly smiled and looked down at baby Brianna. "I think so, too." She stroked the top of the child's head with gentle hands. A mother's hands, naturally soothing. "Clever diapers."

Tom turned toward Shane, his voice beaming of Texas once again. "My son's idea."

Shane shrugged a little boyishly. He had cut an even stack of squares out of the softest quilt he could find. Baby Brianna wore an Aztec print on her little bottom, fastened with safety pins he'd retrieved from a sewing kit.

"Thank you," Kelly said, and he knew she meant for more than just the diapers.

He met her gaze, his voice husky with emotion. "You're welcome."

Tom excused himself to prepare the sofa bed in the front room, giving Shane and Kelly time alone. Neither spoke until the older man closed the door behind him.

"Will you stay here with us?" Kelly asked Shane, shyness creeping into her voice.

Us. She wanted him to sleep next to her and the baby. He wanted that, too. Very much. "Are you sure?"

She nodded, and he stepped forward. "I could find something to make a night cradle out of. It's an old Comanche practice, placing the baby in a cradle between its—" he couldn't very well say parents; he wasn't Brianna's father "—beside its mother."

"That's a good idea," she said, cuddling her daughter. "I'll dress her in one of my T-shirts to keep her warm."

"I'll be back soon." Shane toured the cabin and found a large, sturdy gift basket the realtor had sent Kelly as an apology for the house cleaning delay. He emptied the current contents and removed the handle. Next he padded the basket with the remainder of the diaper quilt, tucking the fabric all around.

Tom reclined in the sofa bed, reading an old magazine. It was still daylight, but the power was off, making the cabin dim. "I left a couple of flashlights on the dresser," he said "And a kerosene lamp for later."

"Thanks, Dad." Shane held up the makeshift cradle. "It's for Brianna."

"She's beautiful, isn't she?"

Shane smiled, recalling the child's soft baby skin and cap of smooth golden-colored hair. "That she is."

He returned to the bedroom to find Kelly waiting anxiously for him, Brianna asleep in her arms. She didn't want to be alone, he realized. She wanted his company, a friend with whom to share the joy.

He placed the basket-cradle beside her, and she lowered Brianna into it. The child stirred, but didn't waken. "I was worried that she was born too early, but your dad said she's fine. Those last few weeks didn't matter."

Shane climbed into bed, settling himself on the other side of the baby. "As soon as the phone lines are restored, we need to call your mom." He tucked the blanket around Brianna when she kicked at it, loosening its hold.

Kelly didn't mention Jason, for which Shane was grateful. Jason would claim Brianna soon enough. He would see the child, and he would want her. Kelly would have a father for her baby—the rightful father.

As an exhausted Kelly closed her eyes, Shane listened for the rush of rain, but the only sound he heard was the soft even breaths of a newborn.

A smile caught his lips. "Hey, little *ona*," he whispered stroking her tiny back. "You sent the storm away." And brought a ray of sunshine into Shane's lonely heart.

He glanced at Kelly. Bordering on sleep, her eyelids fluttered. She was sunshine, too. Pretty Kelly with her scatter of golden freckles and pale yellow hair. He would miss them both—mother and daughter. The perfect family that wasn' his.

Hours later Shane remained awake, cloaked in the dark, the weather outside quiet. He heard Kelly lifting her daughter from the basket. Brianna hadn't cried, but she hadn't nursed yet, either. Shane knew why Kelly reached for the baby.

I shouldn't be here, he thought.

Kelly whispered to little Brianna, something soft and sweet.

Shane closed his eyes. If Kelly needed him would she ask for help?

Help? He swallowed nervously. Why would she need him? Mothers had been nursing their children since the beginning of time. It was instinctual, wasn't it? Shane frowned. He couldn't be sure, especially since Evan had been a bottle-fed baby.

Although Shane's eyes remained tightly closed, he knew Kelly had untied the ribbon on her nightgown, sliding the fabric off her shoulders to bare her breasts.

He tried not to picture her, but couldn't help the image that surfaced in his mind. God help him, but he wanted to remove that makeshift cradle and slide next to her, become a part of something he had no right to share.

A suckling sound filled the room, and he smiled. Brianna nursed eagerly, a healthy, happy baby.

If he offered to stay with Kelly would she let him? Would she welcome his company? He could cook for her while she recovered, tidy the cabin, help take care of the baby. He knew childbirth took its toll on a woman's body. She deserved to rest. And deep down, he wanted to be there for as long as possible. Shane wanted to lie in bed night after night and listen to Kelly nurse her infant daughter.

Seven

At 5:00 p.m. Kelly stood in the kitchen, preparing a cup of tea. The storm had passed, Brianna was seven days old, and Shane had stayed at the cabin. It seemed natural to have him there, eat the meals he cooked, say goodbye each morning when he left for the rescue, relax in the evening together, tend to Brianna.

She stirred a small amount of sugar into her cup. Even sleeping in the same bed with him felt natural. She was, after all, recovering from childbirth, so what harm could come of it? Her nipples ached from nursing Brianna, not from thinking about Shane.

Didn't they?

Kelly pushed away her last thought and the tingle that came with it. Shane was her friend, and their compatible routine was about to end, only he didn't know it yet.

She glanced at the kitchen clock. 5:05. He would be back soon.

He entered the cabin a long time later, longer than she had anticipated.

Edgy from the wait, she snapped at him the moment he crossed the threshold. "Where have you been?"

He closed the door behind him, but rather than respond in the same harsh tone, his voice was patient, a little wounded. "I had some things to do. What's wrong? Has Sunshine been fussy today?"

Wonderful. Now she felt like an ogre. Since Shane was convinced that Brianna's arrival had chased away the rain, he had nicknamed the baby Sunshine. "No. She's been just fine." Her daughter had napped most of the day, a perfect little angel, still asleep in her makeshift cradle. "My mom called."

"Oh." He sat on the sofa. "Did you have an argument?"

"Sort of." Rolling her shoulders, Kelly joined him on the couch. "Mom wasn't too happy when I told her I planned on spending the rest of my maternity leave in Texas. She doesn't understand why I decided to stay here for the next two months."

But Kelly had her reasons. Good reasons. Jason hadn't returned to Ohio yet, so why should she? Besides, being in Texas made her feel closer to Grandpa.

And to Shane, she added hastily, her pulse tripping a little. Shane Night Wind lived in Texas, and at the moment, he lived with her. "Since I won't be going home anytime soon, my mom is coming here instead. She wants to see Brianna."

"That's understandable." He cast his eyes to the floor, studying it as though it held great importance. "I guess she'll be staying with you, huh?"

Kelly nodded. "She'll be here on Tuesday."

"That's only three days away," he remarked, still studying the braided area rug in front of him.

Kelly glanced at her roommate, and he pushed his hands through his hair. In profile, the thick dark mass concealed one eye. It made him look more like Puma—rangy and dangerous. Stunning.

Were they playing house? she wondered. Pretending they had a right to live together, even temporarily?

"Maybe this is better for you," she said.

He lifted his head. "What do you mean?"

She met his gaze and delved into the subject that had plagued her since the storm. "Brianna must remind you of Evan."

He didn't respond right away. Instead he took a deep, audible breath. Kelly heard it catch before he released it.

"Of course she does," he said finally. "But that doesn't mean I can't separate the two. You're my friend, Kelly. I like being here with you and Brianna."

"And we like having you here." Okay, so they weren't playing house. They were friends, a man and a woman who just happened to sleep comfortably in the same bed, her baby daughter snug between them.

Right. As Kelly smoothed her dress, she became even more aware of her tender nipples. What about those awkward moments? The sensual heat that thickened the air?

Like now, she thought. They sat quietly, their breaths shallow, their gazes locked. Shane's hair had fallen forward again, and her bra chafed the fullness of her breasts.

Suddenly she wanted to kiss him—lean forward and press her mouth against his. But she had no business lusting after Shane. She had just given birth to Jason's child. Besides, kissing would only complicate their friendship, especially while they slept under the same roof.

"So where did you go earlier?" she asked, forcing herself to sound normal.

"Shopping." He smiled, his lips tilting like a half-moon. "Wanna see what I bought?"

"Sure." Did he know how devastating that crescent smile was? How boyishly bright and heart-stopping?

He headed out the door, then returned carrying a big, flat box and several plastic bags. After dumping the bags on the barrel chair, he pointed to the box. "It's one of those portable cribs. You know, the playpen type. Brianna certainly can't sleep in that basket for the next two months. She'll be rolling over before you know it.''

The joy in his eyes warmed the mother in her. She stood to examine his gift. ''Thank you, Shane. It's perfect.'' The picture on the box depicted its contents, but his excitement made the gesture even more special. His generosity knew no bounds. He had already supplied a car seat—an item they had used when he'd driven her and Brianna to the doctor three days before.

''I bought more of those little drawstring nightgowns, too,'' he said, reaching into one of the bags to retrieve the pink and yellow clothes. ''Oh, and check this out.'' He lifted another cloth item. ''It's an *ona* carrier.''

Kelly smiled. She liked the way he spiced his sentences with the Comanche dialect. *Ona* in his unusual drawl was a word she had come to know well.

He adjusted the straps, then slipped them over the front of his shoulders. The corduroy pouch rested against his chest. ''I think Brianna's going to like this. Little ones love to be hauled around.''

The baby carrier didn't detract from his masculinity. If anything, it added an air of paternal appeal. But then Shane Night Wind knew all about fatherhood. For six months, a child named Evan had been his son.

''I bought two of these,'' he said. ''One for each of us. That way we won't have to keep readjusting the straps.'' He met her gaze and lifted another pouch. ''This is yours. I thought a tan color would look pretty with your hair.''

And his was deep blue, she realized, a shade that complemented the faded denims he always wore. ''Thank you.''

The forbidden urge to kiss him returned. Kelly swallowed. They had kissed once, over a week ago, yet she could still taste him. He had an unmistakable flavor—exotic, like the blend of his heritage.

Brianna's piercing wail broke the silence. Kelly turned, Shane on her heels. They entered the bedroom at the same time. She lifted her daughter and held her close. Sweet, perfect Brianna. Texas sunshine.

"Is she wet?" he asked.

Kelly nodded, and Shane reached for a disposable diaper. Kelly almost missed the cloth diapers he'd made. Disposable were more practical, of course, and more absorbent, yet wrapping her daughter in homemade diapers seemed fitting somehow.

Brianna fussed while Kelly changed her, the baby's tiny faced puckered with discontent.

"She must be hungry," Shane commented, lifting the child from the bed.

They had fallen into such an easy routine, Kelly thought, tending to Brianna together.

No, not quite together, she amended quickly. Brianna's feedings didn't involve Shane, at least not consciously.

As he placed the baby in her arms, their eyes met.

A lingering stare. Gentle. Intense. Almost sexual.

If she unbuttoned the front of her dress, would he stay? Would he watch the baby nurse?

Kelly's breath hitched. Did he listen at night when she lifted Brianna to her breast? He never stirred during those moments, never said a word. The room, of course, was dark, but the child suckled noisily, greedy for her meal.

"I better go," he said when Brianna fussed even louder.

Kelly only nodded. She couldn't possibly ask him to stay, no matter how much she wanted him to.

Kelly sat in Shane's living room, studying her mother. Why did her mom seem different now that they were away from home? Was it Brianna? Much to Kelly's surprise her mom doted on the baby the way a proud new grandmother should. Not that Linda Baxter wasn't a good person. It was just that she seemed so calm and pretty, not stiff and angry the way she had been before Kelly left for Texas.

Tom leaned forward to coo at Brianna, who lay in a blanket bundle on Linda's lap. Tom and Shane had invited Kelly and her mom for dinner, and now the foursome relaxed in the living room, socializing companionably.

Well, sort of companionably. Kelly hadn't said much and neither had Shane. Their parents had done most of the talking. And smiling.

Kelly cocked her head. Just how many times had Tom and Linda smiled at each other? Good heavens, were they flirting? Her mom and Shane's dad?

Maybe it was her imagination. Her mother wasn't the flirtatious type, nor Tom the man-about-town sort of guy.

But they did look good together. Linda with her petite frame and blond bobbed hair, Tom with his Irish complexion and muscular physique. They were both attractive, yet conservative in their own way.

Tom reached for Brianna, and as Linda handed the baby to him, their eyes met. Kelly glanced down at the floor. How many times had that very same look passed between herself and Shane? This was embarrassing, she thought. Mortifying.

The room hummed, time ceasing in the way it did when two people made the air turn thick. Good grief. Tom and her mother were stealing oxygen—sucking it right up.

While Shane shifted beside her, Kelly studied her shoes. Not that her simple tan flats deserved special attention, she just didn't know where to focus her gaze.

"How about some coffee or tea or something?" Shane said, rising from the rattan sofa, clearly anxious to duck out of the room.

"Coffee for me," Tom responded. "How about you, Linda?"

"Tea sounds nice."

Before someone could ask Kelly for her preference, she hopped up. "I'll give Shane a hand."

She followed him into the kitchen, and he opened the cabinet and removed a large can. While he measured coffee grounds, she set about to make tea. They approached the sink at the same time, but he stopped and motioned her forward. Silent, Kelly filled a small pot and set it on the stove.

Great, she thought. Here they were, friends who had slept in the same bed, yet they couldn't think of a thing to say. She sifted through tea bags, trying to look busy while he placed the coffeepot under the faucet. When he turned abruptly, he bumped her arm. Both jumped from the unexpected contact.

"Sorry," he mumbled, his voice raspy.

"That's okay." More than okay, she decided, as her heartbeat tripped and fell. She missed those accidental touches. The cabin wasn't the same without Shane. It didn't look the same, feel the same. It didn't even smell the same, even though she knew Shane avoided cologne because of its effect on the cats. His scent boasted of nature—soap and water, air, rain, sunshine. Texas elements.

He leaned against the counter, looking rugged and handsome, his clothes sturdy ranch wear. His hair, combed away from his face, hung down his back in a thick, dark ponytail. She had the wicked urge to release it, let it flow into her hands. Would it feel like a waterfall? Cool and luxurious slipping through her fingers?

Kelly glanced at the coffeemaker. The liquid dripped slowly. Shane, too, focused on the coffeepot, his gaze intense. Were they overly aware of their parents' attraction because their own proved difficult?

"So how are you getting along with your mom?" he asked suddenly.

Kelly breathed a sigh of relief. Words, any words, made the moment more bearable. "Pretty good, actually. Of course it's only been three days."

"She's not hassling you about suing Jason?"

"No, but I'm sure she will eventually. Right now she seems preoccupied with being a grandmother."

He smiled. "That's a good thing."

"Yes, it is."

Shane missed Brianna. Kelly could see it in the uneasy tilt of his lips—the soft, sad smile edged with paternal need. Her child had found a place in his heart. He wanted to move back

How to validate your
Editor's FREE GIFT "Thank You"

1. Peel off gift seal from front cover. Place it in space provided at right. This automatically entitles you to receive 2 FREE BOOKS and a fabulous mystery gift.

2. Send back this card and you'll get 2 brand-new Silhouette Desire® novels. These books have a cover price of $3.99 each in the U.S. and $4.50 each in Canada, but they are yours to keep absolutely free.

3. There's no catch. You're under no obligation to buy anything. We charge nothing—ZERO—for your first shipment. And you don't have to make any minimum number of purchases—not even one!

4. The fact is, thousands of readers enjoy receiving their books by mail from the Silhouette Reader Service™. They enjoy the convenience of home delivery...they like getting the best new novels at discount prices BEFORE they're available in stores...and they love their *Heart to Heart* subscriber newsletter featuring author news, horoscopes, recipes, book reviews and much more!

5. We hope that after receiving your free books you'll want to remain a subscriber. But the choice is yours—to continue or cancel, any time at all! So why not take us up on our invitation, with no risk of any kind. You'll be glad you did!

6. Don't forget to detach your FREE BOOKMARK. And remember...just for validating your Editor's Free Gift Offer, we'll send you THREE gifts, *ABSOLUTELY FREE!*

GET A FREE MYSTERY GIFT...

YOURS FREE!

SURPRISE MYSTERY GIFT COULD BE YOURS _FREE_ AS A SPECIAL "THANK YOU" FROM THE EDITORS OF SILHOUETTE

The Editor's "Thank You" Free Gifts Include:

- ● Two BRAND-NEW romance novels!
- ● An exciting mystery gift!

PLACE
FREE GIFT
SEAL
HERE

YES! I have placed my Editor's "Thank You" seal in the space provided above. Please send me 2 free books and a fabulous mystery gift. I understand I am under no obligation to purchase any books, as explained on the back and on the opposite page.

326 SDL C6MD

225 SDL C6L7
(S-D-OS-11/00)

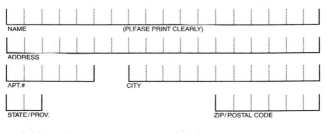

NAME (PLEASE PRINT CLEARLY)

ADDRESS

APT.#   CITY

STATE/PROV.   ZIP/POSTAL CODE

Thank You!

The Silhouette Reader Service™ — Here's how it works:

Accepting your 2 free books and gift places you under no obligation to buy anything. You may keep the books and gift and return the shipping statement marked "cancel." If you do not cancel, about a month later we'll send you 6 additional novels and bill you just $3.34 each in the U.S., or $3.74 each in Canada, plus 25¢ shipping & handling per book and applicable taxes if any.* That's the complete price and — compared to cover prices of $3.99 each in the U.S. and $4.5 each in Canada — it's quite a bargain! You may cancel at any time, but if you choose to continue, every month we'll s you 6 more books, which you may either purchase at the discount price or return to us and cancel your subscription.

*Terms and prices subject to change without notice. Sales tax applicable in N.Y. Canadian residents will be charged applicable provincial taxes and GST.

nto the cabin and share his nights with the baby he called
Sunshine. The baby who reminded him of Evan.

He turned and shrugged. Was he shaking off his emotions?
he wondered. The ones attached to his sleeve?

"The water's boiling," he said.

"Oh." She turned off the burner, her movements jittery.

They prepared a tray, adding store-bought cookies, a small
pitcher of cream, cinnamon sticks and a bowl of sugar cubes.
It looked festive, warmly domestic in a way that made Kelly
ache.

He lifted the tray. "Ready?"

She nodded. They hadn't mentioned their parents, yet both
took a slow, steadying breath, working up the courage to
enter the living room and face the sensual vibrations there.
Guilt, Kelly decided. Guilt over their own forbidden desire—
new mother and a man who had lost a child, using lust to
combat loneliness.

Shane placed the tray on the glass-topped coffee table, and
Kelly noticed Brianna lay in her portable crib, sleeping
soundly.

Tom handed Linda a cup of tea. She thanked him and directed a question to Shane. As they engaged in small talk
about the rescue, Kelly stole a glance at her mom.

Linda sported a beige blouse and brown trousers. She favored natural colors, subtle hues that suited her simplicity. She
wore no jewelry, not even the wedding band Kelly's dad had
placed on her finger a lifetime ago. As long as Kelly could
remember, her mom had been widowed. Although she never
dated, she didn't talk about her late husband, either. She spent
her days as a single mother—hardworking, slightly nagging—
a woman who understood the hardship of raising a child alone.

Kelly frowned into her tea. Would that be Brianna's description of her twenty-four years from now?

Just as the conversation lulled, a loud knock sounded at the
door.

"I'll get it." Shane hopped out of his chair, leaving Kelly
alone on the sofa, mulling over her last thought. Funny how

she had never really analyzed her mother's life before, neve
sympathized with her plight or wondered if she was happy.

When Shane returned, everyone looked his way. Beside hi
stood the most stunning woman Kelly had ever seen. Dresse
in a colorful ensemble of dyed cottons and silk scarves, je
black hair cloaked her shoulders. As she tilted her head, purpl
stones winked at her ears, enhancing the rest of her sparklin
jewelry. Her eyes were as dark and exotic as a moonless nigh
her lips boasting burgundy. She was neither young nor old–
a slim, mystical muse suspended in time.

The lady smiled at Shane, and at that dawning mome
Kelly knew the enchanting gypsy was his mother.

"Grace." Tom left his chair and came forward to hug he
"What a surprise."

Fascinated, Kelly wanted to keep staring, but realized h
curiosity might be interpreted as rude. *It's not polite to star*
How many times had her mom drilled that expression into h
head?

Oh, goodness. Her mom. She turned to see Linda with
frozen smile on her face, sinking a little into her chair. Kelly
heart constricted. Clearly Linda felt bland and boring next t
a woman as brazen and beautiful as Grace Night Wind.

They would endure the introduction, then make a polite b
hasty exit. For once in her life, Kelly wanted to protect h
mom. If Shane's willowy ex had just walked through the doo
she, too, would be eager to escape.

Morning dawned a bright spring day, light spilling throug
the window, birds chirping in the distance. Kelly relished th
moment, the beauty she'd found in Texas. Friendship an
peace. The birth of her daughter.

"Who was on the phone?" Linda asked as she entered th
bedroom, her hair damp from a shower. "I heard it ring befor
I turned on the water."

Kelly finished diapering Brianna and cradled the child
her arms. Brianna smelled of talcum powder and lotion–
clean, sweet baby scent. She stroked her daughter's head an

eleased a nervous breath, hoping her news wouldn't provoke
n argument.

"Marvin called, Mom."

"Your lawyer? What did he say?"

"Jason agreed to take a paternity test. We won't have to
orce him into it."

Linda struck her fist in the air, a quick, triumphant motion.
'Thank goodness. He's back in Ohio, then?"

Kelly shook her head. "Not yet. But he plans on returning
n two weeks."

The older woman sat on the edge of the bed. "Good. That
neans you can go home with me. I'll call the airlines and
ook you on my flight." She tightened her robe when it
lipped open. "We should probably get an extra ticket for
Brianna. We can put her in the car seat between us. If we
on't get an extra ticket, we'd have to hold her through the
ntire flight."

Apparently her mother had already checked with the airlines
bout traveling with an infant. It irked Kelly that decisions
vere being made for her. "I don't want to go home that
oon." She wasn't ready to leave Texas or the peace it offered.
'I'm staying until I have to go back to work."

"I can't believe this." Openly frustrated, Linda pulled a
and through her hair. "That's nearly two months away.
'ou're going to wait that long for the paternity test? You can't
xactly sue Jason for child support if you drag your feet on
ne test, Kelly."

"I'm not dragging my feet. I spoke with Marvin about
nis." And the attorney had been understanding and patient,
reating Kelly in a professional, respectful manner. "Jason can
ave his blood drawn in Ohio, and I can take Brianna to a lab
ere in Texas. There are ways to do this long distance." She
idn't want to rush home just because Jason would be there.
he wanted to enjoy her maternity leave, not fret about what
e was doing and who he was doing it with. "Once the test
esults are in, I'll wait for Jason to contact me." She would
ive him time to accept the fact that Brianna was his, time to

shake off the fear of fatherhood. "I'm not suing him for child support."

"This is insane." Linda raised her voice, then lowered it when the baby let out an irritated squawk. "Do you know how hard it is to support a child on one income? Brianna deserves more. Her father is rich. Why shouldn't he pay?"

Kelly placed the baby in the portable crib, tucking a blanket around her. What Brianna needed was love and tenderness. Jason's money wouldn't give her that. "Mom," she said, lifting her gaze to study Linda's pained expression. "This isn't really about Brianna, is it? It's about you and me, and the things you think I missed out on. The things you couldn't buy."

The older woman blinked, her eyes turning watery. "When you were younger I wanted to give you pretty dresses and fancy dolls, all the finery a little girl should have. And then when you were older, I wanted to send you to college."

Saddened by the catch in her mother's voice, she sat down beside her. "I never mentioned college. I never even considered it."

Linda sniffed. "That's because you knew we couldn't afford it."

Kelly tilted her head. "That's not true. It's because I had no idea what I wanted to do with my life. What would I have majored in? I'm not the brainy type."

"You could have majored in art," Linda said, stunning her speechless.

Art? Her mother thought her drawings were that good? Good enough to plan a career around? Parents didn't encourage their kids to study something as risky as art, did they?

She glanced down at Brianna, at the tuft of blond hair and tiny fingers curled around the blanket. Sweet, perfect Brianna. If her daughter were gifted in music or theater, would she support those gifts? Kelly's eyes misted. Of course she would.

She lifted her gaze. "Thanks, Mom."

Linda met her misty stare. "For what?"

"For loving me."

They both cried after that, cried softly in each other's arms, woman to woman. Kelly closed her eyes and took comfort in the feeling. "I'm going to stay in Texas for just a while longer. I can't explain it, Mom. It's just something I need to do."

Linda stroked her hair. "Then I'll try to understand. Do you forgive me for nagging you all these months?"

"Yes."

The shrill ring of the telephone pulled them apart. Linda, closer to the nightstand, grabbed the receiver before the sound woke Brianna.

"Hello?"

Kelly watched her mom and realized the person on the other end of the line was Tom. Her mother sat a little straighter, spoke a little softer.

"I...um...suppose we could," she said. "Of course, we'd like the chance to get to know her, too. All right, then. We'll be there at two." She paused and said goodbye.

"What's going on?" Kelly asked.

"That was Tom." Linda twisted her hands in her lap. "I accepted an invitation for us. I hope you don't mind."

"We're going to Tom's house?"

She gave a tight little nod. "For lunch. Shane's mother wants to get to know us. She was disappointed that we didn't stay longer last night."

Kelly pasted a smile on her face, hoping to appear more relaxed than she felt. Was Grace Night Wind curious about her or her mother? Or both?

"Lunch sounds fine." But what in the world were they going to wear? All Kelly had were maternity clothes—big, clumsy dresses. "After Brianna wakes up, do you want to check out the emporium in town? Maybe buy a new blouse or something?"

"Why not?" Linda gazed around the room. "We're in Texas. One of those fancy Western shirts might be a nice change of pace."

Kelly's smile turned real. It felt good to have her mom nearby. Really good.

Eight

Shane sat at the table with Kelly, Tom and Linda, waiting fo
his mom to serve lunch. She insisted on handling the mea
herself, refusing the help that had been offered.

"Did I mention my boyfriend is a musician?" she asked
directing the question to no one in particular.

Shane shifted in his chair. "Yeah, a flute player, right?"
His mom had brought her boyfriend into the conversation a
least three times, and Shane was getting a wee bit tired o
hearing about David Midthunder.

"Boy, is he handsome," she went on. "Young, too."

Wonderful. Couldn't she find a man her own age? Someone
with crow's feet and graying temples? Shane didn't like the
idea of his mom dating a guy young enough to be his brother

Grace placed a mixed-green salad in the center of the table
then studied the seating arrangement. "Whose chair is this?"
she asked, indicating the empty seat between Tom and Linda

"Yours, Mom," Shane answered. She did happen to be the
only person standing. Why was she acting so weird? O

weirder, he should say. His mom had always gone her own slightly eccentric way. She didn't walk to the beat of a different drummer. She was the drummer. Or was it bongos she played when he was kid?

Grace squinted. "Linda should sit here," she said, placing her hands on the back of the empty chair. "That way Tom and I can both get to know her."

Linda turned toward Grace. "That's fine. I don't mind moving." She scooted onto the empty chair and placed her hands in her lap. Beside her, Tom picked up his water and took a huge gulp.

Shane glanced at Kelly. She sat staring into her empty salad bowl, a smile quirking one corner of her lips.

Shane raised an eyebrow. Lord have mercy. His own discomfort about his mother's boyfriend had blinded him from the obvious. Grace was playing matchmaker, pushing Tom and Linda together, letting the other woman know that Tom was no longer her type. These days Grace Night Wind had a young musician to tease her fancy.

Satisfied with the current seating arrangement, Grace went back to the stove, her bracelets clanking. Within minutes, she served meatballs in a sour cream sauce with fettuccini noodles, stuffed bell peppers on the side. Her cooking methods were as eclectic as her wardrobe, but Shane appreciated the variety. Her creative meals beat the simple stuff he and his dad normally prepared.

Grace took her seat and said a blessing, thanking the plants and animals, the living, growing things that had made their lunch possible. An old-fashioned Comanche custom, Shane realized, that his modern-day mother hadn't outgrown.

"Tell us about the upcoming fund-raiser," she said, looking across the table at him.

He shrugged. "What's there to tell? We're having one of those big ol' Texas barbecues like we always do."

Grace snorted. "Can't you spice it up somehow?"

Shane frowned. "What do you mean? With like a chili cook-off or something?"

She rolled her eyes. "Spicy, Shane. Artsy, exciting. Different."

"What about an art auction?" Linda said. "There must be wildlife artists who would love to have their work showcased at the rescue."

As Grace clasped her hands together, sterling bangles chimed a merry tune. "Now you're talking. That's a wonderful idea. Isn't it, Tom?" she coaxed, encouraging him to praise Linda's suggestion.

"Yes, it is." He smiled at Kelly's mother, then asked. "Do you know much about art?"

"No, but my daughter does."

All eyes turned to Kelly, and she froze, a fork midway to her mouth. "I...don't," she stammered nervously. "Not really."

"Yes, you do," Shane protested gently, admiring her appearance. A peach-colored blouse highlighted her complexion while a cloth belt cinched her already trim waist. Her hair, fastened high upon her head in a deliberately messy ponytail, made him yearn to touch the loose tendrils framing her face. "You're a terrific artist. The sketches you did of Puma are outstanding. So good, in fact, that I'd like to reproduce them on T-shirts and coffee cups for the rescue. We've got to get the gift shop stocked before the fund-raiser."

Kelly met his gaze. "I'm honored, Shane. Those drawings mean a lot to me. Puma's very special."

And so are you, he wanted to say.

Suddenly the conversation buzzed around them, with Grace putting Kelly in charge of the art auction and herself as head of a jewelry sale that would accompany it. "I'm a jewelry designer," she told Kelly. "That's my expertise."

In one afternoon, the fund-raiser had gone from a West Texas barbecue to a West Texas festival, a blend of color and brilliance, the participants eager to bring it to life.

Shane noticed Linda and his mom sat with their heads together, Linda admiring Grace's emerald necklace, an unlikely friendship dawning.

When Brianna's cry echoed from the guest bedroom, Kelly excused herself from the table and removed a baby bottle from the refrigerator.

Shane studied her through confused eyes. He knew Brianna was being breast-fed. He had lain awake that first week, listening to Kelly nurse her daughter. Night after night, he had immersed himself in the sweet, suckling sound, wishing he could watch.

"Did you wean Brianna already?" he asked, blinking away the fantasy. Thoughts such as his didn't belong in a crowded, noisy kitchen.

"I'm only giving her an occasional bottle," Kelly answered. "Dr. Lanigan said it would be okay. It's easier in public-type places, and by the time I go back to work, she'll be used to the bottle."

So she breast-fed when she was alone with the baby and bottle-fed around other people. It made sense, he supposed. Of course he wasn't an expert on the subject since Evan had been bottle-fed from the start, something his traditional grandmother and career-minded wife used to argue about.

Kelly left the room to tend to her daughter, and Shane scrubbed his hand across his jaw. What kind of man would ask a new mother about her nursing practices? He glanced down at his plate, his appetite suddenly gone. The kind who missed being a father. Missed it in the worst way.

Four days later Kelly stood in front of the beveled glass. The antique mirror reflected her anxious image.

"You look pretty," her mother said from behind her. "You've got your figure back."

Kelly smoothed her dress. It was new, her second purchase from the Western emporium in town. She had even charged a pair of inexpensive cowboy boots to match. When in Rome...she thought, studying herself critically. "How could I have gotten my figure back when I never had one to begin with?"

Linda smiled. "Well, you've got one now, sweetie. Hips and breasts, too."

But not nearly as much as the bombshells Jason normally dated, Kelly noticed. Of course, Jason wasn't taking her to dinner, Shane was. Kelly tilted her head. What kind of women did Shane like? She frowned as the appropriate word popped into her head. Willowy. Long, lean, lithe. Nothing like herself, she supposed.

But then Shane's preference in women shouldn't matter. This wasn't a date, not in the romantic sense of the word. He just thought she deserved a night out. Kelly turned away from the mirror. As much as she appreciated the gesture, leaving Brianna alone for the first time made her jittery.

"If Brianna cries, Mom, promise me you'll pick her up, even if she isn't hungry. I don't believe in letting babies cry themselves to sleep."

Linda laughed. "I wouldn't dream of letting that baby cry. I'm a grandma now, remember? Besides, she'll get plenty of attention from Grace and Tom, too. I asked them to stop by for some dessert. They've been entertaining us almost every night, so I thought it was time to return the favor."

"That's fine," Kelly said. She had seen the way Shane's mom and dad tripped over themselves to get to Brianna. The more doting grandparents the baby had, the better.

Shane arrived before his parents. Linda answered the door and invited him in. Kelly stood back a little awkwardly. Suddenly this felt like a date, especially since Shane wore something other than denim. His pants and shirt were black, separated by one of those fancy Western belts garnished with silver. His hair, combed back into a ponytail, left the angles of his face unframed, displaying raw-boned masculinity and flashing amber eyes.

Linda excused herself and went into the kitchen to check the pie she was baking. Kelly and Shane stood staring at each other. The smell of the warm pastry filled the air, giving the rustic cabin another layer of charm.

"This is for Brianna," he said.

Kelly stepped forward and took the gift bag from his out-stretched hand. She removed the toy and squealed with delight. A stuffed cougar. Now Brianna had her very own wildcat. "This is adorable. Thank you so much."

The gold in his eyes deepened. "Sure. Where is Sunshine? She's not asleep, is she?"

"No. She's just sort of cooing in her crib, making those little bubbling noises. Come on." She invited him to the bed-room, where he leaned over Brianna's portable bed.

"She's such a happy baby," he said, his husky voice wist-ful.

"Yes, she is." Kelly placed the toy cougar beside her daughter, realizing how much Shane missed Evan. It wasn't fair, she thought, that he had been denied visitation rights.

They left the cabin ten minutes later, both in a quiet mood. The drive into town was peaceful, Kelly thought, and the steak house where they now sat filled with Texas magic. The tables were split-log booths, the walls covered with animal skins and Western relics. It was neither fancy nor plain. An establish-ment that belonged right where it had been built—in the lone-star state, on the edge of a tiny town.

The owner's daughter, who also served as their waitress, took their order with a friendly "How y'all doin' tonight?"

When the young woman departed, Shane asked Kelly about the art show.

Being on a fund-raising committee both scared and thrilled her. She had never been involved in anything quite so cultural before. "I've been calling galleries that specialize in wildlife art, and most of them seem eager to get involved." Which made her proud as a peacock. "Of course they understand a portion of the proceeds will go to the rescue, but I assured them the exposure would be well worth it." Shane had a wealthy following, animal activists who appreciated the nat-ural habitats Jungle Hill provided. "I've been in touch with some local artists, too. Nobody famous, just the up-and-coming." But she found it exciting nonetheless.

"You've done all that in four days?" He lifted his water and toasted her. "I knew you deserved this dinner."

"Thank you." Laughing, she clanked her glass against his.

Their salads arrived, so they adjusted their napkins and picked up their forks, still smiling at each other.

"My mom invited your parents over tonight," Kelly told him.

"Yeah, I know." He studied his lettuce for a moment. "But I have a feeling my mom won't make it. She started complaining about a headache before I left."

"Oh." Kelly frowned. "I'm sorry she isn't feeling well."

Shane raised an eyebrow, a wicked slash above his candlelit eyes. "That's okay. I think she's faking it."

The reason behind Grace's feigned headache made Kelly fidget. "She's giving Tom and my mom an opportunity to be alone."

"Yep."

She wondered if Tom was going to kiss her widowed mother. Good heavens. A middle-aged couple kissing while they baby-sat. "It's a little embarrassing," she found herself saying. "They're our parents."

"No kidding. And what about my mom? Miss matchmaker herself."

Grace's bulldozing had them both grinning, then laughing like foolhardy kids. They looked away to curb their adolescent fit, but only ended up laughing harder when they stole a quick glance at each other's silly, tight-lipped expression, knowing it mirrored their own.

By the time dinner arrived, they quit giggling and enjoyed their food, the steaks and company just right.

An hour later Shane paid the bill. "Do you want to go for a walk?" he asked, glancing at his watch. "It's still early." And he wasn't ready to let Kelly go yet. He couldn't remember the last time he'd spent an evening out with a beautiful woman.

She smiled. "A walk sounds nice."

He offered his arm, and when she moved closer, he could

smell the fragrance that seemed uniquely hers. The scent of watermelon and woman—a fresh, thirst-quenching combination.

As they exited the restaurant and stepped onto a crooked sidewalk, a thousand stars winked from the sky. The simple town of Duarte looked prettier with Kelly nearby, the paved highway and street-front businesses giving way to nature. Flowers bloomed and leaves rustled while streetlights and a fairy-tale moon competed for brilliance.

"It's so old-fashioned here," she said. "Like a Western movie town. Or maybe the real thing." She leaned against him. "I almost feel like I've been zapped back in time."

He understood. He felt it, too, touches of the Old West, especially on the corner where they stood, in front of the expansive feed store that served the community.

She pointed to the emporium across the street. "I bought my dress there."

"You look pretty," he responded, turning to study her. "So pretty."

Her voice quavered. "I wasn't fishing for a compliment."

"I know." He touched her hair. She wore it loose, spilling over her shoulders and down her arms. The night loved her hair. A gentle breeze blew it around her face, each long, silky strand bathed in moonlight. She could have been a painting, he thought. An artist's conception of nocturnal beauty.

They glided toward the shadows, both knowing what came next. He lowered his head, and she parted her lips. The kiss was tender, a little shy. A test, he thought, each wondering how far the other was willing to go.

Shane moved closer and deepened the kiss, slipping his tongue past her teeth. He wanted to go as far as she would let him. He wanted to sip from her mouth, then devour it.

Their tongues danced. A mating ritual, he thought, as his body hardened in response. She tasted like the night, like moonbeams and moist flowers. Shane caught her hips and pulled her tight against him. He wanted more than just a taste. He wanted to feed, fuel the fantasy that she had become.

She made a breathy sound, and he felt her fingers skim his face, her breasts press his chest. He imagined them full and creamy, the tips pink and aroused.

They continued to kiss, their mouths fusing then coming apart, over and over. Tender nibbles, little bites, deep tongue thrusts.

Finally they drew apart and stared at each other. A sexual stare in the dark. A vibration.

He brought his hand to her dress and brushed lightly over her breasts. "Do they hurt?" he whispered. Did they ache for his touch, his tongue?

She nodded, and he nuzzled her neck. "I hurt, too," he said, his groin throbbing.

They stayed like that for a long while, in each other's arms, aching for relief.

"Ice cream," he finally managed to say against her hair. "We should get some ice cream." Something cold, something to douse the fire.

"Strawberry," she answered, disengaging herself from his arms.

Shane knew they weren't going to talk about the kiss. And apologizing for it or claiming it shouldn't have happened would be as good as a lie. They both took what they wanted. Not as much as they wanted, but enough to make their blood swim.

"The pharmacy is open until nine. They have a soda fountain." He guided her from the shadows and into the light. Like jewel thieves, he thought, after a heart-pounding heist.

They walked side by side, but didn't touch. No hand holding. No linked arms. Touching proved dangerous. The night held too many shadows, too many secluded spots to slip into. Too many out-of-the-way places to kiss.

The pharmacy was bright, but not overly crowded. They sat in one of the red vinyl booths and looked across the table at each other. Her lips were still moist, he noticed, and slightly swollen from where his teeth had staked their claim. Wind-blown and passionately kissed, she made his blood swim all over again.

"Is strawberry your favorite?" he asked.

She eyed the napkin dispenser. "Vanilla, too. But I'm in a strawberry mood tonight."

Yeah, vanilla was too plain, he thought. Not enough kick to compete with misbehaving hormones. "I'm thinking a chocolate malt. I like that malted flavor." And it was just strong enough to confuse his palette, especially since the taste of flowers and moonbeams still lingered on his tongue.

The soda fountain waitress took their order and departed in crepe-soled shoes, her ruffled pink skirt and white blouse a standard uniform of years gone by. Shane knew her name, had spoken to her often, yet this time he felt almost surreal. "This end of town is more like the fifties than the Old West, don't you think?"

Kelly nodded and reached for a napkin. "Duarte's an unusual place. I can see why my grandpa loved it. He was sort of caught up in the early days. You know, with those old-man suspenders of his."

Shane grinned. "Yeah, Butch was an interesting guy. Ohio and Texas all rolled into one." Kind of like his granddaughter. Kelly wore a Western dress and boots, but Ohio was still there, in her eyes, in the scatter of freckles across her nose.

Darlene, the pink-and-white waitress, brought their milk shakes, then went about her job, wiping down the front counter.

Shane watched Kelly pick up her straw, remove the paper and slip the straw into place. But before she took a drink, she dipped her finger into the whipped cream topping. Smiling, she tasted it.

There was nothing deliberate in her movements. Nothing purposely sensual. They were almost girlish, innocent in a way that had him swallowing back an aroused groan. The fact that she could seduce him without intent was nearly more than he could bear.

He sampled his own drink, but the malt wasn't potent enough. Nothing compared to the taste of a woman. A sweet, vibrant woman named Kelly.

He frowned as another thought crossed his mind. It hadn't taken his mother's matchmaking to bring him and Kelly to-

gether. They had done that all on their own. Of course Grace
wasn't trying to set them up. She wouldn't dream of pairing
Shane with a woman who had ties to another man. His mother
had been there during the fallout of his marriage. She had seen
his pain firsthand. A pain he sure as hell hoped he wasn't in
danger of repeating.

A week later Kelly stood beside Grace on the porch, both
women watching the scene before them. Tom loaded his truck
with Linda's luggage, and Kelly's mom clucked over Brianna,
saying goodbye to her grandchild as though she would never
see her again.

"Everyone looks so sad," Grace said.

"Leaving is always hard." Kelly glanced at Shane's
mother. "I'm glad everyone was here, though. You know,
together."

"Me, too." The other woman sighed. "Tom's going to miss
Linda. He needs someone in his life."

"They live so far away." Kelly watched her mother turn
Brianna over to Shane. He tucked the baby into the cloth carrier he wore, her tiny body snug against his chest. I live so
far away from Shane, too, she thought. None of us are meant
to be together. "My mother never dates. Tom's the first man
who has sparked her interest since my dad, I suppose."

"Yes, she told me. Your mother and I talked about a lot of
things. Our hopes, our dreams. Being single mothers from the
same generation is something we both understand."

"I'm a single mother, too," Kelly said, feeling her eyes
mist. Shane stood beside the truck, rocking his body, lulling
Brianna to sleep. Watching him with her daughter made her
heart throb. In less than two months, they would say goodbye.
Shane would no longer be a part of her everyday life.

"Yes," Grace responded finally. "You are a single mother.
But you're not widowed like your mom." She turned to face
Kelly. "You're unmarried like me."

Kelly gazed into the other's woman's dark eyes and caught
her own reflection. Or at least she thought she did. The familiar image disappeared as quickly as it had surfaced. Grace

Night Wind looked like a gypsy, her jet-black hair blowing in the Texas breeze, sunlight glinting off her jewelry. Could she see the future? Tell fortunes? "Shane said you weren't interested in marrying Tom."

"I wasn't. And that's because I knew I wasn't in love with him." She took Kelly's hand and held it lightly in hers. "Having no man is better than marrying the wrong one. Remember that, okay? Being a single mother isn't such a bad thing."

"It's lonely, though."

"But you shouldn't marry for loneliness. Or for the sake of a child. You should marry for love."

Because the conversation was making her maudlin, Kelly forced a smile. "Since Prince Charming hasn't appeared at my door on bended knee, there's a good chance that I'll be single for quite some time."

"Maybe," Grace said. "And maybe not. The future is impossible to predict. But in the meantime, Kelly, be happy. Live each second as if it's your last."

Wise words from a Comanche gypsy, Kelly thought. A woman who relied on instinct rather than a crystal ball. A beautiful gypsy who had raised a beautiful son.

They stood quietly for a moment, then turned toward the porch steps where they descended together. Linda came forward to hug them both, then accepted Tom's help into the truck. He had offered to drive her to the airport, a man keeping his own emotions in check.

Shane waved as Tom backed up the truck and turned onto the dirt road. Walking over to where Kelly and Grace stood, he slipped between them.

"I'm leaving tomorrow," Grace said. "But I'll be back before the fund-raiser."

Shane nodded, and Kelly looked his way. Brianna's tiny head was barely visible, her golden hair peeking out from the blue cloth. When Kelly's turn came to go home, she would miss Shane Night Wind. Miss him terribly.

Nine

On the following Sunday, Shane, Kelly and Brianna relaxed at the cabin. Brianna lay in her portable bed, a teddy-bear mobile spinning above her. Although still too young to focus on the toy, her reflexes churned like well-oiled machinery. Arms and legs moved, hands waved, feet kicked. Pride swelled in Shane's chest as he watched her.

Kelly sipped a tall glass of sun tea and sent him a contented smile. They were both pretending their friendship would go on like this forever, he supposed.

"Shane?"

"Hmm?"

"Was Tami your first lover?"

His pulse made a quick, unexpected leap. The question could have fallen from the ceiling and he wouldn't have been more surprised. "Does it matter?"

She stirred her tea, clanking the spoon against the glass. "It does to me."

Okay, take a deep breath, he told himself. Friends were

allowed to discuss old lovers. "Yeah, it happened when we were in high school."

Kelly moved closer, and he knew that meant another question would follow. Her eyes locked onto his, keen with interest. "Was it Tami's first time, too?"

"Yeah."

"Was it good? You know, for both of you?"

He shrugged, uncertain of how to answer. "I guess, I mean it was a long time ago. It's a bit tough to remember." Kelly frowned, and he knew he'd said the wrong thing. She wanted honesty, he realized, the candid truth. "Sure, we both enjoyed it. I know I did. I was young and in love. And it seemed as though Tami was, too."

She blew an errant lock away from her eye. "It wasn't like that for me."

"I know." He wanted to grab hold of her flyaway hair, feel it flutter around his fingers. "Did it hurt, Kelly? Did Jason hurt you?" Shane recalled working through Tami's initial discomfort. A woman's virginity, he'd been taught, was a gift, something a man should treasure. Even an eager teenage boy.

"Not really, no. There was a little pain, but that wasn't really the problem. It was just so, I don't know, different than I'd imagined. Our fantasies don't always live up to reality, I guess."

"I suppose not." He stared across the room, depression just a heartbeat away. "You know what was awful for me?" Without giving her time to speculate, he told her, his past surfacing like a dark cloud. "Knowing that my wife felt the need to turn to someone else. Not just emotionally, but sexually. It made me feel so damn inadequate, like maybe I hadn't been satisfying her all along."

She reached for his hand, urged him to look at her. "A woman would have to be crazy to give you up."

The gentleness, the sincerity in her voice had him aching to lay his head against her breast, take comfort in the warmth. "Thank you."

They didn't speak after that. They sat quietly on the sofa

while Brianna cooed and kicked, lost in her own little teddy-bear world.

"Shane?" she said finally.

"Yeah?"

"What do you think is sexy? You know, in a woman?"

Wheat-colored hair, he wanted to say. Freckles and kisses that taste like moonbeams. He shrugged. "I don't know, all kinds of stuff, I guess."

She left the couch and stood beside Brianna's crib. "Do you know what I think is sexy?" she asked, winding the mobile.

Enchanted by her smile, he leaned forward. "No, what?"

"A man who likes children."

"Yeah?" He felt a grin tug at his lips. "Then I'll cast my vote for motherhood."

She shot him a suspicious look. "You're just saying that."

"No. No, I'm not. I'm attracted to everything about it." The changes it left on a woman's body. Rounder hips, fuller breasts, a tummy that pouched just a little. "It makes a woman seem more real. Gentler. Sexy in a subtle way."

Brianna's mobile played a lullaby, a soft, sweet sound that had Shane looking from the baby to her mother. "I didn't get a lot of sleep the week Brianna was born," he said. "I was awake when you fed her. I kept my eyes closed, but I could hear." The rustle of Kelly's nightgown, her soft murmur to the child, the baby's hungry suckling.

Kelly's breath rushed out, and he glanced down at his hands, suddenly shamed. "I'm sorry, I had no right to intrude. Those should have been private moments between you and Brianna." Moments that, through his own loneliness, he had longed to be a part of.

She came to him and knelt at his feet. "I invited you, remember? I wanted you there."

He looked up and into the face of an angel. "Will you kiss me?"

She smiled and touched her finger to his lips. "Handsome Shane."

"Beautiful Kelly."

"Beautiful Kelly."

She climbed onto his lap, and their mouths met, soft and warm and slow. He let her take the lead, let her touch and explore, bathe his bottom lip with her tongue and then sigh into his mouth. The taste of her poured over him like wine, and he felt it seeping into his pores, drugging him.

She rocked her hips. Unconsciously, he thought. A feminine reflex to the masculine hardness beneath her. Her movements were experimental—a curious caress, a timid touch, the scrape of teeth, flutter of an eyelash.

Her first time in charge, he thought, deciding to keep his hands still. He wouldn't push her, wouldn't ask for more. Physically she wasn't ready, the birth of her child still too recent. Emotionally, he couldn't be sure. In her eyes he saw strength, yet vulnerability glittered there, too.

Rather than touch her, he whispered in her ear. She wouldn't understand his words because they spilled from his lips in the Comanche dialect, but his intent was clear. If she wanted him, he would wait.

As Brianna's cry tore through the air, Shane and Kelly startled, then stopped to listen. Their eyes met in understanding. They had come to know Brianna's moods, and the little *ona* craved attention.

"She's only going to get louder," Kelly said.

He touched her cheek. "I know."

Kelly answered her daughter's call, and Shane came to his feet, slightly dazed. The sexual charge had vanished, yet an underlying feeling remained. Tenderness. Human warmth. A bond he couldn't help but feel.

She went about to change Brianna, powder and diaper, then poke the baby's belly with a finger. No longer angry, Brianna gurgled—a sound of pleasure that made Shane smile. For now, Kelly and her daughter belonged to him. And he wasn't about to spoil this moment by dwelling on their upcoming appointment. Next Monday was still six days away.

On Monday afternoon, Shane sat in the waiting area of the hospital lab, hating everything about it. The sea of unfriendly, tired faces, the sterilized smell permeating the halls. But most of all, he hated the feeling, the memories that lingered too close to his heart.

Brianna had been fussy during the drive, and it had been a long, anxiety-ridden trip, one he couldn't let Kelly make on her own. But in spite of that, Shane figured Kelly preferred going to a big, impersonal city hospital. No one would wonder about her there, no one would care that a paternity test was being conducted.

Both Brianna and Kelly were to have blood drawn. Shane understood the process of DNA analysis, and a child's mother as well as the alleged father played a part in it.

Damn Jason Collier anyway. Kelly didn't deserve this.

And neither do I, he thought, recalling another hospital lab, another woman and another baby.

Shane tugged a hand through his hair. "Do you want a cup of tea or something?" he asked Kelly. She sat next to him, holding her daughter.

"No, thank you," she answered, her smile a tad too brave.

He cursed Jason once again, then caught sight of Brianna's tiny face. Her eyes, at half-mast, bore long, luxurious lashes. And her nose—a round, little button, was edged in pink, a remnant from her crying jag. She resembled Kelly, yet she didn't. Shane suspected the cleft in Brianna's chin had come from Jason, and probably the color of her eyes, too.

He touched Brianna's hair. The soft, golden curls slipped through his fingers. He couldn't hold on to the silky locks no matter how hard he tried.

What would it feel like to see yourself in a child? he wondered. To know you helped create a life? Sure, he'd looked for himself in Evan, but what he'd found had been a lie. A manifestation of hope.

"Kelly and Brianna Baxter," a female voice said.

Shane turned. A young woman, a hospital employee, wearing a pastel smock and stark white pants, called the familiar names.

The moment Kelly stood and adjusted Brianna in her arms, the child protested with an agonizing wail, alerting everyone in the room. Kelly cooed and rocked, sending the uniformed woman a nervous smile.

She knows, Shane thought. Brianna knows. He came to his feet, but Kelly halted his plan. "That's all right. We'll go alone," she said.

Feeling useless, he watched her approach the other woman. They disappeared behind a heavy wood door, the barrier muffling Brianna's heart-wrenching cry.

The tired faces in the waiting room went back to their out-of-date magazines. One old man closed his eyes and attempted to nap in his chair.

Since Shane was already standing, he walked around the corner to the nearest vending machine. Reaching into his pocket, he removed several quarters and inserted them into the slot. He chose coffee, even though he knew the strong, bitter brew would burn his stomach.

As the dark liquid dripped into a plastic cup, he heard movement behind him, then the sound of coins jingling in someone's hand. Shane removed his coffee and turned. The man behind him nodded, his face somber.

He returned the nod, then went back to the waiting room. The chair he'd deserted was being occupied by someone new, an elderly lady with bluish-gray hair, so he picked a seat closer to the heavy wood door, intent on being nearby when Kelly and Brianna emerged.

Sipping coffee and clock watching, he waited. And waited.

Had Kelly shooed him away for his own good? Or would it have made her uncomfortable to enter the lab with a man when the paternity of her child appeared to be in question? Maybe the technicians in a city lab weren't any different from those who worked in a small town. Curiosity was human nature.

Damn you, Jason. Damn you all to hell.

When Kelly exited the lab, Brianna whimpered in her arms.

"Hey, little Sunshine." Shane kissed the baby's forehead, his heart heavy.

"She was scared," Kelly said.

"I know." Evan had cried that day, too. "Let's get out of here."

They buckled Brianna into her car seat and headed back to Duarte, the highway a long, lonely road. The child drifted off to sleep, and Shane sighed.

"If you're hungry I can stop at a drive-through," he told Kelly.

"Thanks, but I'm fine."

She stared straight ahead, a bundle of nerves. Hardly fine, he thought. "Are they going to mail you the results?" He knew the procedure, but asked anyway. Not talking about it would only worsen the tension.

"Yes. Once a comparison is made, Jason and I will both receive a copy."

Both. The unity of the word made the coffee in his stomach turn sour. How could Jason ignore Kelly and Brianna once he knew the truth?

"How long did they say it would take?"

"Two to three weeks. It would be quicker if we all would have gone to the same lab, but I prefer it this way. I can keep busy until Jason contacts me."

Rather than curse Brianna's father once again, Shane berated himself. Jason claiming his daughter would be a good thing, yet the idea had Shane gripping the steering wheel in jealousy and despair.

He had lost Tami and Evan and soon he would lose Kelly and Brianna, too. It was only a matter of time before Jason Collier acknowledged what was rightfully his.

In the weeks that passed, spring gave way to summer, bringing drier winds, floral aromas and warmer temperatures. But inside the cabin, Kelly's mind wasn't on the weather. The paternity test results weren't in yet, so she had yet to hear from Jason. Of course on this balmy evening, Jason wasn't occupying her thoughts, either. Shane was.

She fluffed the pillows on the sofa bed. Was it too obvious? Would he know the minute he walked through the door? She glanced over at Brianna. The child lay in a cradle swing, the tick-tock motion her latest form of therapy. The swing, of course, had come from Shane. Another generous gift that would eventually be shipped to Ohio.

Kelly turned back to the bed. She didn't want to think about going home, not now. Not while she planned a seduction.

The knock on the door nearly sent her flying out of her skin. Oh, God, was she ready? Could she really do this?

"Come in," she called out, sparing the bed one last nervous glance.

Shane entered the cabin with a smile on his face, his blue jeans fitting just right. His shirt snapped in front, the buckle on his belt fairly simple. Tonight, his clothes seemed important. And so did hers. She had chosen a cotton dress from the emporium, a cool summer print.

Suddenly he frowned at the bed. Kelly twisted her hands together.

"Have you been sleeping out here? Are you sick?" he asked.

She found her voice, grateful it wasn't as erratic as her pulse. "No. I made it up for us. I figured we could relax and watch the movie."

"Sure, that sounds good," he responded casually. "Sunshine likes her swing, huh?"

"She loves it." Kelly made her way over to her daughter. "It's about time for a bottle, though."

Shane's eyes brightened. "Can I feed her?"

Kelly smiled. "Sure."

Within minutes, the milk was warmed and Shane had Brianna settled in his arms. He sat in the chair near the fireplace, looking far too paternal. Kelly's chest constricted as she watched him. He adored her daughter, and her daughter adored him. Brianna responded to the sound of his voice, the strength of his hands. He represented the father figure in her young life, the man she expected to see.

"Sunshine's starting to doze," he said.

"She didn't nap today, so she'll probably sleep through the night." The baby's unconscious part in the seduction, Kelly decided, her nerves flaring once again.

Shane came to his feet, and Kelly took a deep breath. Seduction? That word sounded much too sultry to apply to her. Too experienced. Too worldly. Too everything, she thought, smoothing her simple cotton dress. Women who seduced wore miniskirts, push-up bras and stiletto heels.

"I'll put Sunshine to bed," he said, shifting the groggy baby.

"Thank you." Kelly kissed her daughter's forehead, then locked gazes with Shane. His eyes glittered in the pale amber light. Did he know how badly she wanted him? Could he tell?

She looked away first. "I'll fix us a snack."

As the popcorn came to life in the microwave, she poured two tall glasses of soda. After the movie, she would ask him to stay the night, share the sofa bed with her while Brianna, asleep in the other room, dreamed of teddy bears and fluffy toy cougars.

I can do this, she told herself. She needed to. Imagining Shane's breath against her cheek had become an obsession. His hands on her breasts, his tongue in her mouth, his...

"Kelly?"

She turned and spilled the soda; it splashed onto the counter in a bubbly pool, the plastic liter bottle bouncing.

"Oh, my goodness." She grabbed a towel, her hands shaky.

"Let me help." He dampened a wad of paper towels and went after the liquid that dripped onto the floor. "Are you okay?" he asked, looking up at her with those metallic eyes. "You seem kind of jumpy tonight."

I'm a basket case, she wanted to say. A woman who didn't have the slightest idea how to offer herself to the man she wanted. "I'm fine. You just startled me, that's all."

Once the spill was properly cleaned, she removed the popcorn and dumped it into a big bowl. "Are you ready for the movie?" She had rented a film Shane suggested, but doubted her scattered brain would be able to concentrate on a science fiction thriller. Two hours seemed like forever at this point, a galaxy light-years away.

He reached into the bowl. "Ready and willing."

A double entendre? Not likely, she thought. He appeared more interested in another mouthful of popcorn than in romance.

He placed their sodas on an end table, removed his boots and climbed into bed. For a moment she just stared. His skin looked dark and rich next to the crisp white sheets, his unbound hair silky against the pillow.

"Shane?"

He looked up and smiled. "Yeah?"

She stood in front of the television, holding the remote control, the VCR power light a small red dot behind her. She couldn't wait for the next galaxy, she had to do this now.

Her breath whooshed out. "I had an appointment with Dr. Lanigan today."

He leaned forward, concern creasing his brow. "Something's wrong, isn't it? That's why you're so edgy."

"Nothing's wrong." She studied the buttons on the remote. "He said that I...that it was fine for me to—" she lifted her gaze and plowed straight into his "—resume sexual activity."

Silence. The absence of sound. Nothing but the pounding of her heart.

Inside the cabin, the air grew thick, warm and heady, like a muggy Southern night. She didn't break eye contact and neither did he. They remained six feet apart, staring at each other.

Kelly locked her knees to keep them from buckling. Suddenly he moved. A jungle cat in his prime, eyes flashing, muscles bunching, crawling to the edge of the bed.

He stopped when he reached her. She stood, motionless, unsure of what to do. What to say. How to breathe. The air in her lungs was trapped.

He placed his hands on her waist. They looked dark against the fabric of her dress, big and slightly scarred. And his hair…that satin-draped hair fell across his shoulders like a waterfall, the low-burning lamp intensifying the subtle auburn streaks. Fire she could touch.

"Are you sure this is what you want?" he asked.

Her fantasy kneeled before her on the bed, and she couldn't breathe. Couldn't talk.

Dizzy, she thought, so dizzy.

"Kelly?" he pressed gently, his gaze never wavering. "Please, I need to hear you say it."

"Yes," she managed finally, the air in her lungs spilling out.

He swallowed, a soundless motion that drew her attention to his throat and the copper flesh just below it. She knew his chest was free of hair, a smooth mass of muscle and sinew. How would it feel to lay her hand upon it? Cover his heart with her palm? Feel the strong, rapid beat?

"What about protection?" he asked, swallowing again.

She tipped forward a little. "I bought what we need." More than they needed. Boxes of condoms, ribbed, lubricated—the choice was his.

"Will you undress for me?" he asked. "Will you let me see you?"

With a quiet nod, Kelly reached for the buttons on her dress and felt herself tremble. Tonight she would deny him nothing. The front of the garment fell open, exposing her bra, a glimpse of her belly. When she slipped the dress from her shoulders and let it pool at her feet, he smiled.

She stood before him in her bra and panties, simple undergarments she had chosen with him in mind—white with a flutter of lace. She was no longer a virgin, but with him she felt pure. Chaste of heart, a young mother he admired.

Moonlight shone through the windows, slashing across the bed in a beam of light. It illuminated Shane in a heavenly glow, melding with an amber hue. He removed his shirt, and when he did, the light bathed his skin. He could have been a sculpture set in bronze, she thought, real yet not. A work of art. Too beautiful to be human.

But he was, she realized. Alive and breathing just for her, his chest heaving from the air that filled his lungs. Hoping to please him, she reached for the clasp on her bra and unhooked it.

Her breasts filled his vision, and he lifted his hands to touch. Lightly, she thought, ever so lightly. He skimmed her nipples with the tips of his fingers, then leaned forward to taste her with his tongue.

A shiver tingled at the base of her spine, and she knew this was what fantasies were made of. The tip of a man's tongue, the scent of his skin, the fever shining in his eyes. Shane Night Wind. She could have dreamed him. A waking dream. A midnight secret.

Her nipples peaked against his mouth. He was careful, she thought, gentle with the part of her that nourished a child. He laved tenderly, kissing as he licked, a rumbling building in his chest.

A masculine purr.

She gripped his shoulders as dizziness swept over her. He purred. Like a cat, only louder. The deep, strong rumble of a mountain lion.

He slipped his hand into her panties. "I want to do this for you," he said, his mouth damp against her nipple. "I want to make it happen."

Kelly shifted her legs. He didn't remove her panties. Instead he kept his hand inside of them, like a naughty teenage boy, his fingers a slow steady rhythm.

She let the sensations guide her—the wave rocking her body, the moonlight kissing Shane's skin, his callused fingers.

She breathed his name and stroked his hair. He lowered his head to her belly, teasing and licking. Lingering.

And then he removed her panties, tugged them over her hips, the wisp of cotton and lace soon forgotten. With masculine fascination, he combed through her curls. She grasped his shoulders and widened her stance, her hips bucking. He put his mouth against her—that hot, sexy mouth.

She bucked again, then looked down at him. He steadied her hips and kissed between her legs. Kissed that sensitive nub while his fingers delved deep inside.

The climax ripped through her hard and fast. Color blurred her vision. Gold, copper, red. His eyes, his skin, the fire in his hair.

Her heart slammed against her ribs, pounding so loud, it thudded in her ears. A vibration. A sound. Sheer, blinding pleasure. She absorbed every flicker of light, every movement. Every flame that doused her skin, every shudder that sizzled through her system, then left her weak and mindless.

Was she on the bed? She gazed around the room, but couldn't see through the haze fogging her eyes. She reached out and connected with flesh. Hard, muscular flesh.

With a dazed smile, she blinked him into focus. Shane. Alluring Shane. The man who had made it happen.

Ten

Her freckles looked like fairy dust, he thought, golden lights sprinkled across an upturned nose. Her hair fell across the pillow like a tangle of wheat, and creamy breasts swelled and peaked into rosy crests.

He skimmed her tummy and smiled. It was trim, yet slightly pouched. The declaration of motherhood pleased him. As did her dazed expression.

"You're still wearing your jeans," she said.

Shane nodded. Being clothed while she was naked felt strangely erotic, as if he held her magic in the palm of his hand. If she had wings, she wouldn't fly away. At least not tonight. Tonight she would stay beside him, bathed in the afterglow of an orgasm.

"Kelly?"

"Hmm?"

"Where's the protection?"

She smiled a little shyly. "Under the bed. There's...um...a few choices."

He smiled back at her and reached beneath the sofa. Locating the condom boxes, he opened one and secured a foil packet. He didn't have a preference, but her careful selection had him grinning like a randy schoolboy. "You can take my jeans off now."

In response, she worked free his buckle and tossed the belt over the side of the bed. His zipper came next. He bulged beneath it, anxious for her touch.

She didn't disappoint. She reached into his boxers and stroked him, rubbed her thumb over the tip. Losing himself in the sensation, he kissed her. A long, slow, agonizing kiss.

She seduced him, this enchanting woman, this elusive butterfly with her imaginary wings and warm, gentle hands. She had taken the power back, the magic, and he was caught in her spell. He needed to be naked. Needed to feel his aching flesh against hers.

"Take them off," he growled, pressing his lips to her ear. She smelled like summer, fresh-cut watermelon and flowers that grew wild. Damn if he couldn't taste her.

As she tugged at his jeans and the boxers beneath them, their mouths came together in animalistic fury. Flesh against flesh, they rubbed and kissed, their teeth scraping, tongues diving. He wanted to devour all of her, every curve, every feminine swell. Their legs tangled around the sheets as they rolled over the bed, hungry for each other.

He tore open the foil packet, then braced himself above her. Lifting her hips, he sank into her, his penetration deep. She closed around him—warm and wet, all woman, creamy and sweet.

So good, he thought. So damn good.

When he felt himself teetering for control, he pulled back to look at her, stroke her cheek, count her freckles. Slow down, his mind said. Don't go too fast. Don't let this end too soon.

Sheathed inside of her, he didn't move. He stayed where he was, poised above her, gazing into her face. And then time stood still, trapping his soul in shadow and light.

How could he miss her when they breathed the same air?

How could he long for her when their bodies were already joined?

As though answering his questions, she smiled, the tenderness in her eyes a sudden balm. She brought her hands to his chest and caressed him, sculpting his form. Intrigued and aroused, he watched her. She skimmed his belly, then slid her fingers into the nest of hair that surrounded his sex. He refused to blink, refused to lose sight of her. She touched him where they mated, fascinated by the closeness, he thought. The unity.

Now was all that mattered, he realized. This moment.

Shane rocked his hips, intent on loving her, giving them both the pleasure they craved. Her kissed her. Everywhere. Her face, her neck, those luscious pink-tipped breasts. She moved with him, danced his erotic dance, ran her fingers through his hair.

The pressure built, that wonderful high that came with human arousal. They rode the wave together, and when he felt himself falling, slipping into that climactic abyss, he clasped her hands and held tight.

Their mouths met, and on her lips he could taste the ocean, the depth of his need, the warm, woozy liquid surging through his veins. He kissed her hard, then flung back his head, gripping her hands, pulling her with him.

He heard her call his name, a siren's call, a seduction. He answered with his body, with heat and hunger—a lethal, maddening orgasm that pushed him deeper. Deeper into the sea. Deeper into pleasure. Deeper into the woman beneath him and the emotion he saw in her eyes.

Spent, he collapsed in her arms, his mind quiet, his body almost boneless. Turning his head, he breathed against her hair, inhaling the floral scent. Flowers, he thought, wild, tangled vines.

"I wish we had forever," she said.

Shane sighed. Wishes were daydreams, a long way from reality. He shifted onto the bed, releasing her from his weight. Forever, they both knew, wasn't possible. "What made you plan this?"

She flexed her body, expanding imaginary wings. "Because I wanted you, and because something your mother said made sense."

"My mother?" Curious, he raised an eyebrow. "Now what could that be?"

Kelly turned and smiled, smoothed the hair that fell across his forehead. "She said to live each second as if it was my last."

"I see." That made sense, he supposed. And seconds weren't forever, but rather fleeting moments of time. His new lover would be gone by the end of the month. "I'm glad you planned it." Rolling back on top of her, he kissed the tip of her nose. "And I think we have enough protection to last a while."

She wiggled her nose. "I didn't want to get the wrong kind. I've never bought condoms before."

"I know." And that pleased him, he realized. "Do you want to take a shower with me?"

She chewed her bottom lip, looking far too innocent for her own good. "Right now?"

"Yes, ma'am," he answered, anxious to see her slick and wet and hungry all over again.

Kissing through the steam, they washed each other, warm water pelting their skin. He explored every inch of her, then let her choose the protection. While she rolled the ribbed latex over him, he waited—hard and hot and greedy. Pulling her close, he took her mouth. She wrapped her legs around his waist, and he thrust into her, deep and full.

When they were depleted and panting in each other's arms, they dried lazily and stumbled back to bed. She put on her panties and bra, so he slipped into boxers and ignited the remote. The VCR tape lit up the television screen with flickering images. She snuggled in the crook of his arm, and while he watched the movie, she fought heavy eyelids, then finally succumbed to sleep.

Beautiful sleep, he thought, touching her cheek. Beautiful Kelly.

An hour later, Shane dozed while the movie played, falling and waking endlessly. Hearing a strange noise, he squinted at the TV, then realized Brianna cried in the other room.

Blinking and rubbing his face, he went to the kitchen and opened the refrigerator door. Groggy, he searched for a bottle, but found none. Waiting a minute to his clear his head, he entered the bedroom and lifted Brianna. Uncertain of what else to do, he carried the baby, snug in a blanket and whimpering for a midnight meal, to her mother. Kelly had expected Brianna to sleep throughout the night, but apparently the baby had other ideas.

Kelly woke instinctively and reached for her daughter, clearly accustomed to the slumber-deprived routine. Shane turned, but her words stopped him.

"Stay with me," she said. "With us."

While she nursed the baby, he sat beside her, a sheet draped across their hips. Brianna rooted at Kelly's nipple, and Shane watched with a sense of belonging. On this moonlit night, they felt like a family, and he knew without a doubt, that for as long as he lived, he would never forget this moment, this woman or this child. Kelly and Brianna would be a part of him forever, even when the Texas sun still shone and they were gone.

The following morning Kelly made herself a cup of tea while Shane and Brianna slept. She carried the steaming brew into the front room and stood quietly to study them. After her meal last night, Brianna had fussed for attention, so Shane and Kelly had kept her in bed with them. And now in the light of day, Brianna snoozed against Shane's broad chest, her padded bottom in the air. Even in sleep, he handled the child gently. One long, muscular arm held her lightly, keeping her tiny body in place.

Kelly sipped her tea and glanced back at the envelope that had arrived in the mail. Somehow she had known it would come today, so she had dressed and walked to the street-front box, breathing the fragrant air, telling herself it shouldn't matter. But it did, of course. If she received the results, then Jason must have, too—discovering, without a doubt, that Brianna was his.

When would he call? When would he make a decision about his daughter? She set her tea on the end table where last night's uneaten popcorn remained. How could she be so confused? So emotionally careless? Wanting Jason to claim Brianna, yet losing her heart to Shane. Little by little she was falling in love, and she had no idea what to do about it.

Shane stirred. Opening his eyes, he looked down at Brianna and smiled. Kelly watched as he lifted the sleeping child and placed her in a snug corner of the sofa bed. Brianna scooted forward on her own, butting her head against a pillow.

Shane met Kelly's gaze, and they shared a smile, the kind adults reserved for puppies, kittens and babies.

"How are you doing?" he asked, his night-tousled mane falling over one eye. That happened often, she noticed, his one-eyed likeness to Puma.

"Fine." She toyed with a button on her blouse. Did he remember purring last night? Probably not. The sound had seemed instinctual—unconscious eroticism. The reminder sent a tingle up her spine. He had purred in the shower, too. Warm water, scented soap and Shane's deep, sexy rumble. "Would you like some breakfast?"

"Sure. Do you happen to have any coffee?"

"I still have some from last time you stayed here." Condoms and coffee. Shane essentials. "I'll start a pot."

"Great. I'll put Sunshine in her own bed."

Kelly nodded appreciatively. "Thank you."

"She's really wiped out," he commented as he lifted the child.

"I guess she should be. She was up most of the night." Kelly glanced at the envelope she'd placed on the TV stand, hoping Shane wouldn't notice it. Brianna's biological father seemed like an awkward subject to broach on their first morning after.

When he left the room with Brianna in tow, Kelly grabbed

the envelope and stuck it in her purse. By the time he returned, she had a pot of coffee brewing. He came up behind her and kissed her neck. She leaned into him as he held her, fear coiling in the pit of her stomach. How could she leave? Survive without him?

Kelly took a deep breath. Did she have a choice? She had a life in Ohio, a job, a home with her mother. Shane wasn't making promises. She was the one who had invited him to her bed, not the other way around.

Suddenly his touch hurt. The kind of pain that came with loss. A deep, dark lonely ache. "I should get breakfast going."

She slipped away from him and went about cracking eggs and frying slices of ham. Shane poured himself a cup of coffee, and although she didn't turn around, she knew he stirred two teaspoons of sugar into it, followed by a dash of milk. She had no idea how Jason prepared his morning coffee or if he drank a second cup by midday.

They sat at the scarred dining table, she fully clothed, Shane in frayed jeans and little else.

He poured ketchup over his eggs, and Kelly imagined them like this for the next twenty years, sleeping together every night, sharing breakfast each morning. He would look much the same, she decided. Perhaps a bit more mature, a touch of gray in his hair and tiny lines around his eyes, additions that often made men more attractive.

"Kelly?"

She blinked and cut into her ham. "Yes?"

"What are you thinking about?"

The ham nearly slid off her plate. "Nothing, really." Just you and me and a lifetime together.

He studied her for a long, drawn-out moment, and she worried he could see the truth in her eyes, the love, the hope, the fantasy of forever. Avoiding his gaze, Kelly lifted her fork and brought it to her lips.

"Why didn't you tell me the test results came in?" he asked just as she swallowed a bite of honey-baked ham that suddenly lost its appeal.

He had seen the envelope, she realized, and had been waiting for her to confide in him. "Does it matter? We both know what it says."

Shane pushed away his plate. "Yeah, but now Jason knows, too."

Had he lost his appetite? She stole a glance at his breakfast and felt the weight of her heart, a treasure sinking to the bottom of the sea. His food was nearly gone.

"You're going to hear from him, Kelly. It won't be long." Shane pushed at his plate again. "That's what you want, right? For him to take an interest in Brianna?"

The question wasn't fair. Of course she still hoped Jason would contact her about Brianna; he was the baby's father. But on the other hand, she had fallen in love with Shane. Fallen hard. "I want what's best for my daughter," she said, answering the only way she knew how. "Brianna will always come first."

The days that followed were hectic. Preparations for the fund-raiser were in full swing, with Shane's mother arriving to help. But Shane decided a break was in order, so he asked his mom to baby-sit Brianna while he whisked Kelly away for a few enchanted hours. The sun shone in a vast blue sky, a perfect afternoon for what he had in mind.

Kelly slanted him a sideways glance, looking like a bright-eyed little girl. She sat beside him in the truck, her hair in twin ponytails, a familiar butterfly barrette restraining bangs that had long since grown out.

He turned onto a narrow path, the four-wheel-drive handling the rough terrain. They rode up a small hill, the only access to their final destination. He had instructed Kelly to dress comfortably—jeans and safe, sensible shoes.

He maneuvered the vehicle in between some dense foliage and parked. "We have to walk from here."

He strapped on a backpack and led her up the hill. "This isn't walking, Shane," she said. "This is hiking."

He chuckled. "Yeah, but it's worth it. Besides, it's not far."

Once they reached the appropriate spot, he pointed to the valley below. "That's where we're going, Kelly. You can't get there by car."

"Oh, my." She stood beside him, clearly awed.

Shane smiled. The rainy season had done just what he'd expected: nourished the ground so wildflowers grew as far as the eye could see. In another area, trees huddled together, providing a natural haven for squirrels and nesting birds. "Let's go."

He started down first, then reached up to help her. The grade wasn't as steep as it appeared, but Kelly handled the descent carefully—mindful, he noticed, of the scattered brush and loose stones. When they reached the bottom, they stepped onto a carpet of flowers.

"This is so beautiful," she said, a light breeze fluttering the hair that escaped her barrette. "Heaven on earth."

Shane nodded. "I used to come here a lot." He took her hand and guided her toward the copse of trees. "But I've never brought anyone with me before." He needed to tell her that, he realized. Needed her to know how special she was to him.

As they walked across the field, he breathed the fragrant air and tried not to dwell on Kelly's impending departure. He would enjoy this day with her, this quiet, beautiful day. "Sometimes I picture my ancestors here," he said. "You know, when the Comanche used to roam this land on horseback."

"Before they lost it," she said.

"Yeah." He supposed the spirit of his ancestors tied him to West Texas, restoring in him what they had fought so valiantly to keep. Pride. Honor. Hope.

Hope? He shook his head. He would lose Kelly as surely as the Comanche had lost Texas. No amount of hope would change that. Destiny had sealed his fate. Her child belonged to another man, and his experience with Tami had taught him a painful lesson—biological bonds weren't meant to be broken. His only recourse was to step back when the time came.

And it would come. Jason Collier would contact Kelly. Of that, Shane felt certain.

They reached the copse of trees and ducked inside. The leafy branches provided shade, but slats of sunlight peeked through, creating a small, magical forest. Clusters of flowers spotted the ground, their colorful blooms growing toward the light.

Shane opened his backpack and unrolled a large, beach towel. Kelly sat cross-legged on one end and he on the other, a carefully selected lunch between them. He knew how much she enjoyed picnics, and today he wanted to please her.

"The chicken came from the deli in town," he said, as he began unwrapping aluminum foil and opening small, plastic containers. "But I did the rest." Simple things he knew she appreciated. Cheese squares and whole wheat crackers, raw vegetables and ranch dressing, chilled grapes and watermelon. The watermelon balls, he supposed, were for himself. Tasting the ripe melon was like kissing her, running his tongue along her flesh.

She loaded her plate. "It looks wonderful. Thank you." Glancing up through the trees, she sighed. "I can imagine your ancestors here, too. Even feel them, like spirits in the wind."

Such poetic words, he thought, such beautiful sentiment. "Do you know who Quanhah Parker was?"

Kelly titled her head. "The name sounds familiar."

"He was the last free war chief of the Comanche." Shane reached for his soda. "He was my idol when I was a kid. He was part white, and for me it helped to know that a famous chief was a mixed blood. Especially at a time in history when half-breeds were looked down upon."

Kelly scooted a little closer, picking at her food delicately. "Who were his parents?"

"You mean which one was white?" He opened the cola and took a swig. "It was his mom. Her name was Cynthia Ann Parker, and she was captured by the Comanche when she was a child. But she wasn't mistreated. Instead she was adopted into the tribe."

"So when she was older she married one of their chiefs?"

Shane nodded. "Yeah, his name was Wanderer. Supposedly they were really close. Madly in love as some folks prefer to tell it. Of course like all great love stories, theirs ended tragically."

Kelly glanced up at the trees again. Searching for spirits, he supposed. Lonely lovers drifting through the sky. "What happened to them?" she asked.

"Cynthia was separated from Wanderer and their sons when she and their baby daughter were captured by the Army and returned to her white family. But by this time, Cynthia didn't fit into the white world anymore. People either pitied her or thought she was odd."

"Did she ever see Wanderer or her sons again?"

"No. They searched, but never found her. Wanderer lost hope and died from an infectious wound. The younger son died, too. Only Quanhah lived to tell the story."

Kelly's eyes turned watery. "What happened to Cynthia and her daughter?"

"The baby took ill and died, and after that Cynthia didn't last long. Some reports say she died of a broken heart. Others claim she starved herself to death." Shane dropped his shoulders. "Either way, Quanhah was left to carry on alone and fight for what he believed in."

"Your childhood idol," she said, blinking back tears.

"Yeah." He set his plate aside. "I'm sorry, Kelly, I didn't mean to make you cry."

She rubbed her eyes. "I'm fine. Just oversensitive, I guess." She reached for her plate, encouraging him to do the same. "We should be enjoying our lunch."

They ate in silence. Neither, it seemed, sure of what to say. Shane drank his cola and tasted the chicken while she sipped water and nibbled on crackers and celery sticks.

A butterfly winged by. Shane turned his head and watched it light upon a nearby flower. "It looks like your hair barrette," he told her.

She touched the ornament, then dropped her hand self-consciously. "When I was a child I used to sit in my mom's garden and study them. The symmetry of their wings, the way they flutter. They're beautiful, don't you think?"

"Yeah." Like her, he thought. Delicate and beautiful. "You still look sad, Kelly."

"I do?" She brushed cracker crumbs from her lap. "Honestly, I'm fine."

She wasn't, he decided, and neither was he. They were missing each other. Sharing the sunshine and missing each other. It made no sense.

He moved their plates out of the way and reached for her. She sank into arms and made a sniffling sound.

"Don't cry," he said.

She buried her head against his shoulder. "I'm not."

But she was, and it made him ache inside. "I need you," he whispered, knowing she needed him, too. Their time together neared its end, and on this bright summer day, he wanted to make memories. Thoughts and images. Sensations.

He reached for the buttons on her blouse. She sat back on her heels, then stilled his hands, opening the blouse herself. Shane watched her, his body growing hard in response.

Instead of removing her bra, she released the cups. It was a nursing bra, making access to her breasts a simple, erotic task.

Reaching out, she brought his head forward, inviting his touch. Accepting her offer, he licked her nipples, tasting and teasing. She made a soft sound of pleasure and held him there.

"Shane." Kelly caressed his cheek, her voice breathy. Aroused.

When he looked up and saw her watching, her eyes glowing with promise, he raised his head and kissed her. Kissed until they melted together like wax, their bodies warmed by the sun, their hearts beating in unison.

She undressed, stripped away the barrier of her clothes while he undid her hair, releasing the ponytails. Only the butterfly remained, the delicate ornament.

She could have been a forest nymph, he thought. A beautiful

reature with pale skin and tangled hair, fairy dust dancing
round her.

She unbuttoned his jeans and freed him, then lowered her
mouth.

To experiment. Learn how to please a man.

Drive him mad with desire.

When he was dizzy, glassy eyed and desperate, she reached
into his pocket and removed the condom he always carried,
the protection that would keep them safe.

Slipping it on, she kissed him, openmouthed and carnal, her
tongue diving down his throat. He met her ravenous onslaught
with the same voracious need, then pulled her onto his lap.

Smiling, she impaled herself, taking him deep, stroking his
length. Shane caught his breath. She rode him, slow and rhyth-
mic, the motion a smooth, liquid current.

The world around them stilled. There was nothing but the
pounding of their hearts, the hunger in their bodies, the taste
of each other on their tongues.

She quivered, and their eyes met. He could see her losing
control, rocking deeper, wanting more. He raised his hips and
thrust into her, increasing the tempo, challenging her stroke
for stroke.

She met his maddening pace, her hair a wild mass around
her shoulders. It cascaded over her face and across her breasts,
tangling like vines.

Together they tripped and stumbled, wildflowers sweetening
the air, the world tilting on its axis. She grabbed hold of the
earth, and while they shuddered through a mind-shattering orgasm, she spilled a handful of dandelions into the air.

They fluttered around Shane like feathers from an angel,
guiding him to Heaven in one slow, sliding motion.

Gloriously spent, he closed his eyes and let the feeling
sweep him away.

Eleven

While Brianna napped in a guest room at Shane's house, Kelly sat across from Grace at the kitchen table, guacamole and chips between them, virgin strawberry margaritas on the side. They had been working diligently on the fund-raiser, comparing ideas, notes and final decisions.

Kelly scooped a chip into the chili-seasoned avocado dip and savored the flavor. Mexican food was a rare treat. As was her involvement in the fund-raiser.

Grace sipped her frothy drink. "Isn't it great not having the men underfoot? Girl time is important."

Kelly enjoyed having Shane underfoot, but appreciated Grace's sentiment just the same. Girl time meant guilt-free snacks and easy conversation. "I wish my mom could have gotten time off to help with the fund-raiser. Her boss is so stingy."

Grace tucked her hair behind her ears, unmasking a striking set of earrings, silver that offset her bronze complexion and onyx that matched her eyes. "Linda's not just your mom. She's your best friend, isn't she?"

Kelly nodded. She didn't need to stop to think about her answer. Linda Baxter was the constant in her life, the woman she could rely on. "But we don't always see everything eye to eye. She's a little more opinionated than most female friends would be, but I guess that's the mother-daughter relationship coming into play."

"That it is." Grace stirred her drink and smiled. "My mother had the tendency to poke her nose into my affairs, too."

Kelly bit into another chip. She recalled how conservative Shane had said his grandmother was, and since Grace was anything but conservative, the disagreements that must have existed between them wasn't hard to fathom.

"My mother called me a hippie, but I thought of myself as New Age. She didn't understand my lifestyle, but in spite of that we were still friends. We lived together for over forty-five years. We shared everything, including Shane. He's the man he is today because we both raised him."

"He's a wonderful man." The man Kelly could picture forever with. The man her heart had given itself to. "But he seems a little more traditional than New Age, though."

Grace laughed. "Yes, well, my mother, God rest her soul, certainly left her socially-proper mark on my son. But then again, Shane has a daring side, too. A dance-naked-in-the-woods, bring-a-mountain-lion-home sort of attitude that most people wouldn't understand."

"Yes," Kelly agreed, hoping her cheeks didn't look as hot as they suddenly felt. She knew all about being naked in the woods with Shane—making love while the trees surrounded them like an enchanted forest.

Grace stood, a red dress flowing to her ankles. "Why don't we go to my room. There's something I'd like to show you."

Kelly followed Shane's mother down the hall and into the bedroom where the other woman often stayed. Although the furnishings were stark and masculine like the rest of the house,

Grace's presence shone through. A colorful scarf was draped over a straight-back chair, and a tangle of jewelry glittered on a practical oak dresser.

She opened the closet and removed an article of clothing. "It's a perfect blend of New Age and traditional. Don't you think?"

Awed, Kelly studied the deerskin vest. A floral pattern of seed beads decorated the leather, lending traditional Indian appeal, whereas buttons made of semiprecious stones added modern flair. "It's incredible."

"I thought so, too. Try it on, Kelly. I bought it for you."

"Oh, my." She reached for the vest and held it against her. "I've never owned anything like this before."

"Well, then it's time you did."

Grace dug through a case of carefully packed necklaces while Kelly removed her blouse and slipped on the vest. Studying herself in the mirror, she smiled. The leather clung to her like a second skin, the buttery feel cool and sensual.

Grace came up behind her. "Look at you." Slipping a choker around Kelly's neck, she fastened it and stepped back.

Kelly touched the delicate necklace. It was stunning in its simplicity—deerskin with a single beaded flower.

The other woman fluffed Kelly's hair, sending it flying wildly about her shoulders. "You're a very beautiful girl."

"Thank you. This makes me feel beautiful."

"Wear it at the fund-raiser," Grace said. "An artist like yourself should make a statement."

Months ago Kelly wouldn't have thought of herself as an artist, but these days she did. Shane had driven into the city to pick up the gift-shop items that bore her drawings of Puma. Later this afternoon she would see her work exhibited on T-shirts, coffee cups and a commemorative poster.

"Thank you so much, Grace."

"You're welcome, honey."

Kelly hugged Shane's mother, wishing she could reveal her heart. But how could she tell Grace Night Wind that she had fallen in love with Shane when she was still gathering the emotional courage to tell the man himself?

Kelly worked beside Shane in the gift shop, stocking shelves and setting up displays. He munched on red licorice while he unpacked a box of stuffed animals, and she eyed the strawberry-flavored candy with disciplined longing. The chips and guacamole had been enough junk for one day. As a nursing mother, Kelly thought it only fair to eat a mild, well-balanced diet, and candy and chili-spiced foods didn't fall under that category.

Focusing on the stuffed toys instead, she grinned. She had convinced Shane to purchase them for the gift shop, and now that she saw their sweet, fluffy faces lined upon a shelf, she knew her instincts had been correct. What parent could resist them? Brianna adored the cougar Shane had given her; she curled up beside it every night. Maybe Brianna needed a toy tiger, too. And a leopard with a pink bow. A girl leopard, Kelly thought.

Shane looked up and caught her planning her daughter's zoo instead of pinning T-shirts on a corkboard display wall. Of course she had already stared at the shirts with a sappy expression, marveling at her drawings, imagining them being worn by strangers.

"Sorry. I'm being kind of lazy," she said.

"No, you're not. You've been working nonstop for weeks. It's okay to get a little dreamy eyed."

Dreamy eyed. If he only knew about her daydreams, the fantasies of love and commitment that involved him. "Those toys are awfully cute."

"Yeah. We should get Sunshine one of each."

Kelly's heart bumped against her chest. His *we* almost sounded like a commitment. How would he react if she told him how she felt about him?

Maybe she should do it right now. Spill her soul. Let it pour out.

She chewed her lip. Then again, maybe she should wait

until after the fund-raiser. A few days after, when the stress levels associated with it lessened.

"I wonder if Sunshine will get attached to a special blanket," Shane said, musing out loud. "Puma has one. Heck, he's still crazy about it."

Kelly blinked, then stared for a moment, assessing his odd comment. Not about her daughter, of course. Children often acquired a fondness for a particular blanket or toy. But cougars? "Puma has a security blanket?"

"Sort of, yeah. It's an old saddle pad he fell in love with at his original home. And when he came to live with me, it came with him."

"What exactly does he do with it?" she asked, trying to picture a hundred-and-eighty pound cat dragging a security blanket behind him.

"When he first moved into the cabin with me, it helped keep him calm. He would sit on it and tread, then nurse and purr like crazy. He'd pretty much stay wherever his sucky was placed."

Kelly grinned. "His *sucky?*"

Shane shrugged, then laughed a little. "I had to call it something. Besides, he made this sort of chewy-sucky noise when he nursed on it. The name seemed to fit."

The more she heard about Puma, the more she adored him. "And how does he react to his sucky now that he's older and living outdoors?"

"Covets it mostly. He keeps it hidden in his lockdown." Shane flashed a telling smile and leaned forward. "But when I wash it for him, sometimes I notice the corners are spit-soaked, like he still sucks on it once in a while."

Kelly studied her lover's expression, the emotion she saw in his eyes, the same glittering pride that often shone for Brianna. "The relationship you have with him is amazing. The way you talk about him, he seems almost human."

"But he's not," Shane responded, his voice serious. "We lived together successfully because Puma decided I was another cougar. A tall one who walked funny, I suppose. But a cat just the same." He picked up one of the stuffed animals and stroked it. "Most exotics either mark you as predator or prey. There's nothing in between. You're either one of them or you're not."

And Shane Night Wind was definitely one of them, she thought. "Did he ever bite you?"

"In the beginning, yeah. I was pretty much covered with bruises, but eventually he learned roughhousing wasn't acceptable. I suppose he thought I was a grump most of the time—this ugly cougar who never wanted to play." Shane met Kelly's gaze, then smiled. "He didn't give up easily, though. He was always trying to figure out ways to sneak in a bite."

"How?" she asked, thoroughly charmed. If Shane was an ugly cougar, then a beautiful one didn't exist.

"Sometimes when I was standing near him, he would yawn really big. Kind of nonchalant. You know, like it wouldn't be his fault if my arm just happened to fall into his mouth."

Kelly couldn't help the spurt of laughter that erupted from her chest. Shane joined her in the merriment, and when their laughter faded, they stared at each other.

A stare that intensified the longing in her heart.

"We should get back to work," he said.

"Can't we take a short break instead? Maybe visit with Puma?" Suddenly Kelly needed to be near the cougar, the animal that shared its medicine with Shane. "I'd go by myself, but I know you have strict rules about guests roaming the grounds unescorted." Although she had been permitted out there a few times by herself, on those occasions, she had studied Puma from an artistic standpoint. Today was spiritual. She wanted the cougar to see her and Shane together. Wanted Puma to know that they were lovers.

Kelly pushed her hair away from her face. Was that possible? Would Puma sense a change in her relationship with Shane? Or was it wishful thinking on her part? A romantic notion that a wildcat would know the difference?

"Sure," Shane said. "We can take a break."

As they headed toward the compound, she slipped her fingers through his, giving in to the urge to keep him close. To her, even the simple act of holding hands strengthened their bond. It made them seem more like a couple. Two people who belonged together.

What would he say when she told him that she loved him? Kelly glanced at his profile, that gorgeous angular face. Maybe he already knew. Shane had learned long ago how to read other people's emotions, tap into their energy field. He claimed he wasn't psychic, but he was gifted just the same.

Kelly relaxed her grip. If he already knew, then there was no reason to worry, to cling too hard. Desperate women did desperate things, making doormats of themselves. Hadn't she done that with Jason? Let him abuse her affection? Well, she sure as hell wouldn't let him hurt Brianna. Jason Collier was going to treat his daughter with kindness and respect.

When they reached Puma's habitat, Kelly stood back while Shane greeted the cougar through the metal fence. Shane would help her deal with Jason, wouldn't he?

Of course he would, she decided with a slow, steady breath. A man like Shane would never abandon the needs of a child. Or the woman who loved him.

She looked up to see Puma staring at her with that lone eye, his tawny frame crisscrossed by the security fence. She stepped forward and stood next to Shane, her concentration focused on the cat.

"I wish I could touch him," she said softly.

"I can't let you," Shane responded just as quietly.

"I'm aware of that." But a part of her couldn't help but wonder if she would be considered friend or foe. Prey or predator.

Puma moved closer to the edge of his enclosure as he let out a loud *"oooow,"* and Kelly realized he had just said hello. Friend. It was the same greeting he had given Shane only moments ago. Excitement bubbled in her chest.

"Hi," she said in return. "I'm Kelly. I'm the one who looked like I had a watermelon in my tummy. Only it was actually a baby. I named her Brianna."

Clearly amused, Shane shot her a sideways glance. She smiled and looked back at Puma. The cat made a similar noise, only this one quieter, more personal.

An odd feeling came over Kelly. She couldn't enter Puma's cage and she couldn't touch him, yet he seemed to be asking why she had come.

To tell you that I'm in love with Shane, her mind answered.

Puma assessed her with his eye, that one golden beam of light. Kelly shifted her feet. This was silly, she thought, expecting a cougar to carry on a telepathic conversation. She turned toward Shane, and as she did, Puma made another noise. Stunned, she turned back.

This time the cat's throaty call sounded remarkably like a long, drawn-out ''I *knoooww*.''

The fund-raiser was in full swing, the smell of a deep-pit barbecue drifting through the air. The picnic area of the rescue bustled with activity as volunteers filled the serving table with side dishes and salad fixings. A party tent housed the art show and a large exhibitors' booth displayed cases of hand-crafted jewelry. The other temporary booths provided carnival-type games, offering family fun and novelty prizes. While a local band played country cover tunes, adults and kids alike strolled in and out of the gift shop, their Texas attire blending into the festive atmosphere.

Shane couldn't have asked for a better turnout. Friends and neighbors lent their support as did the corporate sponsors and wealthy animal activists whose generosity helped make the rescue a thriving facility.

Shane adjusted Brianna in her carrier. She rode like a backward kangaroo, her face resting against his chest, tufts of hair peeking out from the pouch. He had offered to baby-sit since Kelly manned the art show and he roamed the grounds, free to socialize, playing the role of the proper host, no matter how foreign it still felt to him.

He scooped his arm around Brianna, balancing her in the carrier as one of his sponsors approached. Nelson Pickles

stood a good foot shorter than Shane with thinning yellow hair
and wire-rimmed glasses. Shane figured the quiet millionaire
had been considered a nerd in his youth, thus his preference
to animals over people.

"Hello, Shane," Nelson said in his nasal twang, extending
his hand. "It's good to see you."

He shook the other man's hand. "You, too. I hope you're
enjoying yourself." Their conversations were usually sparse
as neither forced the other to engage in party talk. Shane knew
the drill. Nelson would stop by the fund-raiser, say hello, then
send a sizeable donation the following week. Asking for
money made Shane uneasy and he suspected Nelson understood his discomfort, even respected it. Their relationship
might be unusual, but at least there was no pretense.

"What do you have there?" Nelson asked, indicating the
blue pouch.

Shane removed the little girl from the carrier and adjusted
her red-and-white gingham dress. Smiling, he said, "This is
Brianna Lynn."

Nelson studied the child curiously. "A human baby."

Apparently Nelson had been hoping for a clinging monkey
or a frisky cub. Shane supposed that was where he and the
other man differed. Babies, no matter what their species or
gender, pleased him. He delighted in having a daughter as
much as he had enjoyed having a son.

As soon as the weight of his last thought hit him, he ago-
nized over the blunder, blinking back his pain. Brianna wasn't
his daughter any more than Evan had been permitted to be his
son.

"I bought a painting," Nelson said.

"You did?" Still struggling with his emotions, Shane
placed Brianna against his shoulder so she could peer over it.
She gurgled and grabbed hold of his hair, signaling her ap-
proval. She smelled soft, like lotion and powder—a gentle
creature tucked in cotton, ribbon and lace. "I'm glad to hear
it. This is the first time we've gotten the local galleries involved, so your patronage is certainly appreciated."

"It's an interesting piece. Wildlife art has always been my favorite." The other man straightened his bolo tie and excused himself before their conversation faltered. "I think I'll go sample some of that barbecue, then be on my way."

"Be sure to say hello to my dad. I know he'd like to see you."

"Will do." The millionaire gave Brianna's shoe a quick pat and disappeared into the crowd.

Shane shifted the baby, cradling her in his arms. She looked up at him and stared—that funny, perplexed gaze babies seemed to have down to a science. Her little eyebrows furrowed, and he grinned. "I guess you haven't quite figured me out yet, huh? Me or my friends."

She studied his grin, kicked her feet, then smiled back at him, telling him she had figured him out just fine, even if the jury was still out on his friend.

"Hey there!"

Shane took a deep breath, preparing for twenty-questions as Brianna's head bobbed in the direction of the greeting. Barry Hunt, the bulbous-nosed owner of the One Stop Gas Station and Mini Mart lumbered toward them, a gossip-induced gleam in his eye. Another offbeat friend, he thought, wondering what Brianna would think of this one.

"She's a cute little bug, ain't she?" Barry flashed his gold tooth. "'Course it's obvious she ain't yers. You with that dark skin and all, and her being pink-faced and blond."

Great. Shane tried not to scowl. Just what he needed, another reminder that Brianna wasn't his. "I never claimed she was."

"True, but everybody in town knows yer dating her mother."

If everybody knew, it was because Barry had told them. Shane ran his fingers through Brianna's hair, the silky wisps of golden curls. Then again, he had taken Kelly out to dinner, kissed her in public, driven her to Dr. Lanigan's office. And in a small town like Duarte people were bound to notice. "Kelly's a good friend."

"How come the baby's father's ain't in the picture? He dead or something?"

"No, he's just a fool." Lying to Barry wouldn't do any good and neither would avoiding his questions. Being evasive would only encourage the old codger to gossip even more.

"Well, it's nice of you steppin' in like you have." Barry's white hair and full beard made him look a little like Santa Claus at a Texas hoedown. "I was raised in a boy's home. My mommy and daddy were both fools."

Which meant, Shane assumed, that the old guy had been unwanted and unloved. Growing up tough and ornery might have been Barry's only defense. Faulting him for it now didn't seem fair. "Kelly's going home next week. I didn't step in forever."

"Maybe you ought to," the old man said before he spotted Martha Higgins looking his way. "There's a lady waiting on me, son. I'll catch up with you later."

With a bounce in his stride, Barry made his way over to the widow Higgins, leaving Shane staring after him. *Maybe you ought to.* As if it was just that damn simple.

Shane glanced down at Brianna and felt his heart tug. She stared up at him with those bright blue eyes. The baby who had chased away the storm. "You have a daddy, Sunshine," he whispered. "And it's only fair to give him a chance. I gave Tom a chance and he turned out to be a fine father."

As Shane headed for the art show tent, he acknowledged his guests, clusters of people eating and drinking, their lives seeming carefree. At the moment, Shane's was anything but. Playing the proper host wasn't easy when losing Kelly and Brianna occupied his thoughts. But asking Kelly to become a permanent part of his life would be like signing his own emotional death warrant. Sooner or later Jason would enter the picture, and Shane would be pushed by the wayside.

He carried Brianna into the tent and scanned the art-show arena for Kelly. Spotting her in the thick of things, he brought Brianna next to his face and nuzzled her cheek, inhaling her sweet baby scent. "There's your mommy." Looking like she was right where she belonged, in butter-soft deerskin and feminine jewels, surrounded by painters, gallery owners and patrons of the arts. Kelly had taken to the fund-raiser like a mermaid to the sea, fitting in eloquently with the money crowd. It wouldn't be long before Jason Collier saw this side of her, too. In no time, the Ohio heir would realize her potential as a social companion. A beautiful, young society wife. The mother of his child.

Shane kissed Brianna's cheek, the pain almost too much to bear. As he approached Kelly, the baby made a happy crowing sound and flapped her arms, excited to see Mommy.

"Hi." She greeted them both with a radiant expression, reaching for her daughter. Brianna bobbed her head and bumped Kelly's nose, making Kelly laugh and kiss her—a sweet smacking kiss right on the lips. The little girl blew bubbles and gurgled, then smiled that chubby baby smile, the one that dimpled her chin even more.

Shane knew that in another month Brianna's smile would turn to a broad grin, then soon after that, laughter. Her sensory and motor skills would continue to develop, but he wouldn't be there to see any of it. Brianna Lynn would grow up without him.

A lump formed in the back of Shane's throat. Brianna was only two months old. She wouldn't remember Texas or the man who wished he was her father. The man who had no claim upon her.

"When are you scheduled for a break?" he asked Kelly, knowing she and his mom had secured a throng of university art students to help out.

"Soon." She bounced the baby, her eyes filled with excitement. "I'm having so much fun, Shane. We've sold so many paintings, and the Wild Winds Gallery even offered me a job if I ever needed one."

"That's great," he said, forcing the air from his lungs. She wouldn't need a job in Texas. Jason lived in Ohio, and he could afford to buy Kelly her own gallery if she wanted one. Tomorrow, Shane thought. Tomorrow or the day after Jason would call. He could almost hear the telephone ringing in his mind, hear Kelly answering it—a premonition he couldn't stop, couldn't interfere with no matter how much he wanted to.

When Kelly's relief arrived, Shane led her outside and toward the food. He had spent most of the afternoon chatting with his sponsors and now he intended to have lunch with Kelly, covet her while he still could.

They filled their plates, then found an empty table, taking turns holding Brianna while they ate. The baby appeared to enjoy the festivities, the breath of color, music and art.

"Your mother's boyfriend is nice," Kelly commented while bouncing her daughter on her lap. "Don't you think?"

"Yeah." Shane had to admit his mom's younger beau seemed like a decent guy. A lively match who fit right into Grace's unorthodox world.

Kelly reached for her drink and sipped, keeping Brianna snug against her. "Your dad's been awfully quiet, though. Sort of alone in a crowd."

"I noticed that, too." And he understood it well. Tom missed Linda and being around hordes of people made that loss even harder. His father had developed deep feelings for Kelly's mother, even if their time together had been short. It took a lonely man to recognize another, Shane thought. A man who knew when the right girl wasn't meant to be. "Dad doesn't get into these fund-raisers all that much. Neither one of us is the party type. We do this because we have to." Shane took another bite of his meat and pushed away the melancholy that threatened to ruin the moment. "But you're having a good time, aren't you, Kelly?"

She nodded and smiled, her hazel eyes bright, her hair glistening in the sun. "The weather's perfect, the food's wonderful and there are people walking around wearing T-shirts with my drawings on them. That makes me feel special."

You are special, he thought, aching to touch her. "What about the music? Do you like the music?"

"It's terrific." She tilted her head toward the country notes, a Western ballad drifting through the air. "Very Texas."

"Then dance with me," he said. "You and Brianna." Shane wanted to hold both of them—mother and child.

She met his gaze, her smile tagging his heart. "We'd love to."

They walked to the grassy area where other couples danced. With the baby between them, they swayed to the music. Lulled by the motion, Brianna closed her eyes and slept against her mother's shoulder. Shane moved a little closer to Kelly, then bent to nuzzle her hair. She smelled like watermelon, the fresh, cool scent he had come to expect. The scent that made him hungry.

Needy. Aware of his body and what it wanted.

"Can I visit you tonight?" he asked.

She turned her head until their lips brushed. "Yes," she said, the word a whisper against his mouth.

"No matter how late it is?" he pressed.

This time her response came in the form of a kiss, warm and full of promise.

Shane slipped into the taste, the flavor he craved. The night would be theirs. Moonbeams, wildflowers and lovemaking until dawn. And when it ended he would ask Kelly for nothing more.

He would keep her and Brianna locked safely in his heart, and when Jason Collier called, he would send them home to the other man. Back to Ohio, where they belonged.

Twelve

Kelly had been excused from cleanup duty because Brianna required a long, quiet sleep, exhausted from her lively day. So she had come back to the cabin, bathed and nursed her daughter, then put Brianna to bed in the front room, nuzzled beside the toy cougar.

Kelly stretched and smiled. Her cougar hadn't arrived yet. He was probably still breaking down booths and packing carnival supplies.

Fighting heavy eyelids, she sat on the edge of the bed and reached for a book. She had agreed to "no matter how late," and she intended to keep that promise by staying awake. Tonight she needed Shane as much as he appeared to need her.

Need was a good word, she thought. A sexy word.

Forcing herself to read, she scanned the pages, but couldn't make sense of them. Her mind was elsewhere. She was naked beneath her nightgown, and the silky fabric felt erotic against her skin. Like the flutter of Shane's hair when he kissed her.

Giving up on the book, she placed it back on the nightstand

stead she would close her eyes and think about Shane, imag-
e his mouth and his hands, that long muscular body.

She fanned her hair around the pillow. Fantasizing about
im wasn't wrong. He was the man she loved. The man who
uched her in secret places and made her moist and warm
side.

Ready.

She shot up like an arrow and looked across the room,
atching her reflection in the mirror. She was ready now, her
air mussed, her eyes glassy, her nipples protruding against a
my gown. And the heat, she thought. The heat between her
gs. The fire fantasizing about Shane had ignited. Yes, she
as ready.

Lowering herself to the bed once again, she let his image
ll her mind. Those gold-flecked eyes, that dark, auburn-
reaked hair. The muscles that shaped his body, the tight
rso, narrow hips. Full, aroused sex.

Soon, she told herself. He would be there soon.

Turning down the three-way light, Kelly remained in bed,
ashed in a pale glow, thinking about her lover. And as she
ctured him leaning over her, his hands lifting her nightgown,
e slept.

And then dreamed.

Her dream felt so real, so alive. He smelled like the night
r, like Texas at midnight, the elements clinging to his skin—
e grass that grew wild on the plains, the flowers that dotted
nyons, the jagged rocks that formed the hillsides.

Warmth radiated from her apparition. A breath upon her
eek, an erotic whisper.

"Kelly."

Upon hearing her name, she fluttered her eyes, caught be-
veen wake and sleep. "I'm dreaming."

"No, sweetheart, it's me."

Me, her mind said. Him. She knew who fueled her subcon-
ious, her fantasy. "But I dreamed you. I'm dreaming now."

"No," the voice said, his tone deeper, less of a whisper.
I'm real."

She felt her hand being lifted, placed upon a solid objec
Groggy, she moved her fingers, then laid her palm flat. A
man's chest, warm and smooth. A heartbeat, strong and steady

"Shane?" She opened her eyes and forced her vision t
focus.

His hair fell over his shoulders in a thick curtain, and h
shirt was open, his jeans unfastened. The light sent shadow
across his face, hollowing the ridges beneath his cheekbone
even more so. His lips looked full, a slight smile tugging a
the corners.

Sexy, she thought.

"I fell asleep," she managed to say. "I tried to stay awak
but I couldn't."

"That's okay. I still have a key." He stroked her cheek, h
fingertips a slow, hypnotic movement. "It's late. After two.

She wanted those fingers everywhere. All over, stimulatin
her. "You smell good. Like the outdoors."

"All I could think about was getting my work done so
could see you." He lowered himself onto the bed, placing h
body next to hers. "I need you, Kelly."

Need. Yes, she liked the word. The feeling. Awake an
aware now, she trapped his gaze. "I fantasized about yo
Shane. I imagined you touching me."

He made a throaty sound, a raw primal noise. Skimmin
her shoulders, he asked "Did I touch you here?" When sh
swallowed and nodded, he slipped his hands down the fron
of her gown and cupped her breasts, rubbing his thumbs ov
the tips. "And here?"

Her nipples peaked, hard and aching. "Yes."

The game continued. He removed her nightgown and let th
air flow over her skin. "Did I put my mouth on you?"

Kelly kept her eyes open, wanting to watch her own sedu
tion, her fantasy come to life. "Yes."

He kissed her nipples, then teased them with his tongu
licking until they were moist and pink. Trailing kisses dow
her body, he stopped at her quivering navel. Slipping work
roughed hands beneath her, he lifted her hips.

"And did I touch you here, Kelly?"

"Yes."

"With my tongue?"

She gasped through an aroused breath. "Yes."

He lowered his head and licked her, teased with his fingers and his mouth. It excited her to admit that she had fantasized about him. It made her feel wanton and free, a woman comfortable with her own sexuality. A woman who wanted more.

She delved into his hair and pressed herself against him, rocking her hips, knowing a climax was near.

"Shane," she said his name as the first shudder slammed through her. It pulled her under and into a current of sensation. Fresh blinding heat.

The rest became an edgy blur—a haze of color and passion, moans and labored breaths. He didn't stop until she clawed his shirt and tugged, ripping the fabric as she pulled him up.

She wanted him naked, hot and hard and taking her to the next level. She reached for his jeans and saw that he was as desperate as she. The gold in his eyes shone like shards of amber glass, jagged and dangerous. She yanked the denim down his hips, felt the silk of his erection spring against her belly. She grabbed hold and stroked, greedy for masculine flesh.

They tumbled into each other's arms, kissing and nipping, never getting quite enough. He grabbled for the protection she kept in the nightstand, knocking the drawer off its hinges as he fisted the foil.

He tore the package, cursing and fumbling, kissing her while he sheathed himself with the condom.

"Look at me," he said, his voice a husky pant. "Know it's me."

She met his gaze and caught her breath. Yes, it was him. Her dream, her reality. Kelly clung to him as he drove himself into her, praying the depth she saw in his eyes was love.

Focusing on that prayer, she let herself believe it was true. For Kelly, living without Shane Night Wind didn't seem possible. Slowly and very surely, he had become her world.

* * *

The morning sun spilled light across the bed, cloaking Kelly in warmth. Shane lay beside her, six foot plus of gorgeous, rumpled male. She reached out to touch his hair, brush it from his face.

His lashes fluttered before he opened his eyes and squinted at her. "Please say it isn't time to get up yet."

She scooted closer. Since she had already risen to feed Brianna, she wore a nightgown and panties. Shane, on the other hand, was still naked. "How about almost time?"

When he stretched, the sheet fell just below his navel, exposing a shadow of hair. "Does that mean it's almost time for breakfast, too?"

Kelly's gaze strayed to the masculine sight. She could see through the outline of the sheet that he was hard. A condition, she supposed, that happened to most men first thing in the morning, whether they had female companionship or not. "Breakfast could be arranged." She wanted to touch him, slide her hand beneath the covers. But it wasn't necessarily sex she was after. She longed for familiarity. The feeling that he belonged to her, that she could touch him anytime, day or night. She wanted to wake beside him every morning, watch his muscles bunch and flex, hear his husky voice.

"We can make breakfast together," he said. "You don't have to wait on me."

Together sounded perfect. "Okay."

He rubbed his eyes and braced himself against the headboard "I don't know how you function without caffeine."

She berated herself for not starting a pot of coffee. Shane drank coffee every morning, and if they were going to have a life together, then she needed to provide a sense of familiarity for him. Small, simple luxuries he could appreciate.

Kelly sighed. She wasn't fooling herself that their situation wasn't complicated or they didn't have a lot to discuss. Technically she still lived in Ohio. And then of course there was Jason. But as far as she was concerned, Jason was an obstacle they could overcome. Times had changed. People these days were married and divorced, had children with other partners. The family from the fifties didn't exist anymore and neither did living by those old-fashioned standards.

Kelly studied Shane's morning-after appearance. Did he love her? He must. He wasn't the sort of man to use a woman—make love to her, then toss her aside. This wasn't an affair. It was more. Much more. What they shared came from the heart.

"I guess you didn't get much sleep," she said finally, re-calling his comment about caffeine.

He grinned at her, his smile lopsided, his hair tousled, the sheet still draped low on his hips. Morning-after suited him. "I'm not complaining."

"I didn't think you were." A tingle, warm yet edgy, shot up her spine. Why couldn't she tell him that she loved him? Say it easily rather than fret about how to broach the subject?

Because he still seemed like a dream, she thought. Too good, too beautiful to be true. Her cougar. Her Comanche knight. An apparition her subconscious had conjured.

She rubbed her fingers over his chin just to be certain he was real. The whiskers were only slightly abrasive, but they chafed her skin just the same. Kelly's nerves settled. The contact felt good. Right.

He caught her hand and kissed each finger. Pleased with his reaction, she smiled. They belonged together. Now and al-ways. "Are you ready to tackle breakfast?"

"Aren't you going to feed Sunshine first?"

"I already did. She was up about an hour ago."

"Oh."

Disappointment dulled the gold in his eyes, and she knew he wanted to watch her nurse the baby, sit beside her and listen to Brianna's sweet little suckling sounds. But there would be other nursings, even other children, she decided. Shane would want more babies, wouldn't he?

He leaned over the bed and grabbed his jeans and boxers from the floor. "Can I use your shower after breakfast?"

"Of course." As Kelly watched him dress, she swallowed,

her mouth suddenly dry. He was still a little hard, not enough to hamper the fastening of his jeans, but enough to make her want him. Maybe she would join him in the shower later, let the water sluice over them while she wrapped her legs around him. Tight, she decided. Tight around him.

Once they entered the kitchen, he made a beeline for the coffeemaker, and she chastised herself for having forgotten again. "How about an omelet?" she asked.

"That's fine. I'll be right back."

He left the coffee perking while she removed eggs, milk and cheese from the refrigerator. When he returned, he kissed her—a warm, spicy kiss flavored with cinnamon mouthwash.

"Hey, that's my brand," she said, laughing when he nipped her ear.

"I forgot my toothbrush. I guess I'm not much good at sneaking into a woman's house in the middle of the night."

Yes, she thought. She could get used to this. Dream-induced sex and domestic compatibility. She glowed from both.

Halfway through breakfast the phone rang. Kelly dashed into the bedroom to answer it before the noise woke Brianna. The baby still slept in the front room, but the sound carried.

"Hello?"

"Hi, Kelly. It's Tom. Is Shane there?"

"Sure. Just a minute." She went back into the dining area and called Shane to the phone. "It's your dad."

While she stood nearby, he took the receiver. "What's up?" Glancing at the alarm clock, he cursed. "I'm sorry. I didn't realize it was so late. I'll be right there."

He hung up and dragged his hand through his hair. "I was supposed to help my dad load the U-haul. We've got to get the tables and chairs back."

"I understand." And she remembered the party-rental place had been overbooked this weekend, making pick up and delivery impossible. "Did your mother and her boyfriend leave already?"

"Yeah, they took off last night. My mom has another jewelry show coming up."

He shoved on his socks and boots, then located his wrinkled shirt on the floor. Kelly noticed it was torn. "I'm sorry," she said, recalling how she had practically ripped it from his body.

He grinned, then shrugged. "That's okay. It's old anyway." He gave her a quick peck on the cheek. "I better go."

She followed him to the front door. He rushed out, breakfast and the impending shower forgotten. Kelly looked down at Brianna, who stirred in her sleep. When the phone screamed again, she went sailing back into bedroom, wishing the cabin had come equipped with a cordless telephone. Apparently Shane's dad was in an impatient mood.

"Tom," she said the moment she picked up the receiver. "Don't worry, he's already on his way."

"What? Who's Tom?" a masculine voice asked.

Kelly's heart slammed against her ribs. She knew immediately who the person on the other end of the line was. "Jason?"

"Hello, Kelly. Your mother gave me this number. She said you're in Texas."

"That's right." He sounded so calm, so civilized, yet her voice vibrated. "Did you receive the results of the paternity test?"

"That's why I'm calling. I'd like to arrange a meeting with you. When are you returning to Ohio?"

"Next week."

"Will you contact me when you get back?"

"Yes, of course." Why couldn't she catch her breath?

"We'll go to lunch. Just the two of us."

And Brianna, she thought. "That's fine, Jason."

"All right. I'll see you soon."

He said goodbye and hung up, his cool, aristocratic demeanor clogging her lungs with confusion. She was sleeping with one man, yet had a two-month-old baby with another. Suddenly her situation seemed immoral. Dirty.

She sat on the edge of the bed and struggled to breathe. She needed to see Shane. Needed him to hold her, tell her that he loved her, soothe her fears, confirm that their relationship was based on more than sex.

Love wasn't immoral, she told herself as she forced air from her lungs. And Shane loved her, just as she loved him. They just hadn't spoken the words yet.

Clinging to that thought, she headed back to the kitchen to clean up the breakfast dishes. Shane would give her advice about Jason, and he would understand if Jason wanted to become a part of Brianna's life. He would think it was the right thing for the other man to do.

Just as Kelly turned on the faucet and filled the sink, Brianna woke with an angry wail. Kelly dried her hands, then answered her daughter's call. Lifting the baby, she rocked gently, quieting the child instantly. It would be hours before Shane returned. Hours before she could tell him about Jason's call.

"We'll just have to keep busy," she told Brianna, who stared at her with eyes the color of Jason's, and a smile so sudden, so tender, it reminded her of Shane. Some traits, Kelly decided, had nothing to do with genetics. Nothing at all.

At dusk Kelly arrived at Shane's house. She parked her rental car and removed Brianna from the baby seat. Shane sat on the porch waiting for her. She had called ahead and asked if they could see each other. He looked tired, she thought, but then he had worked a long day—loading party supplies, driving into the city, then returning to Duarte to resume his chores at the rescue.

Kelly carried Brianna up the porch steps, and Shane stood to greet her. His hair, loose and damp, fell past his shoulders. Apparently he had found the time to shower after all. He smelled faintly of soap, water and a simple, masculine shampoo.

He reached for Brianna, and the baby waved her arms, anxious to be held by him. His dark skin intensified the child's fair coloring; her hair seemed blonder, her eyes bluer.

Kelly sat in one of the weathered chairs and watched Shane do the same.

"What's going on?" he asked, although he sounded like he already knew.

Something in his voice, she thought, a tightness, a pain. A guarded emotion she couldn't quite fathom. A tone that frightened her suddenly, made her think of dark and lonely places.

"I heard from Jason today," she said, shaking off the feeling of doom. Shane cared about her, loved her. He would make everything all right. "Jason called right after you left this morning."

He let out a quick, audible breath. "I've been expecting this. And I've thought a lot about it." He combed his fingers through Brianna's hair with a touch that seemed distant, almost detached. Afraid to feel. "What did he say to you?"

"He asked me to call him when I get back to Ohio." Something was wrong, terribly wrong. Shane was supposed to be her best friend, her lover, her confidant, yet their conversation was strained. "He received the test results and now he wants to have lunch."

"That's good," he responded, his Texas drawl only vaguely familiar. "You should go back early. There's no point in waiting until next week."

A ball of pain exploded in her chest. No point? "What are you saying?" she asked, even though she knew. Dear God, she knew.

"It's over for us, Kelly. What we had isn't important now." He trapped her gaze, his eyes brown instead of gold. "It's time for both of us to move on. Brianna belongs with Jason, and so do you."

Kelly fought back the threat of tears. She didn't love Jason. It was Shane she wanted—the man who just sliced her heart in two. Did he know she was bleeding inside? Or didn't he care?

"Jason didn't even ask about the baby. Not even her name."

Shane rocked Brianna in a slow, mechanical motion—a

movement so unlike him. "He already knows her name. It was on the test results, wasn't it? And that's why he called. To make things right."

She looked up at the sky. The setting sun still shone, blending into a sea of color—red, gold, mauve and a bright stream of blue. It was beautiful, but she hated it. Suddenly she hated Texas, and she wanted to hate Shane, too. He had used her, and now she felt cheap and immoral. Sick inside. She should snatch her baby and run, but Brianna cooed in his arms, fisting a strand of his hair. Brianna couldn't let him go, and neither, God help her, could Kelly. She still loved him.

"Kelly?"

She turned. "Yes?"

"If Jason asks you to marry him, promise me you'll consider it. Brianna deserves to have her birth legitimized."

She went numb, stiff and cold. Her only defense, she thought, to keep herself from breaking down into racking sobs, from shaking until she collapsed. "Please don't presume what's best for my daughter."

He glanced down at the child in his arms. "I'm sorry. I just want both of you to be happy. To have the things you deserve."

Things, she thought, inanimate objects Jason's money could buy. "How noble of you," she said, her words tasting as bitter as they sounded. "To let us go so easily."

"That's unfair." His features twisted, but he kept his tone level. "This isn't easy for me, Kelly. I—" His voice cracked, and her heart jumped.

Say you love me. Please, Shane. Say you love me.

"It just isn't easy," he continued, maintaining control of his voice again. "But we both knew it would end. Neither one of us talked about forever. Jason was always there, like a ghost between us. He's your destiny, not me. He's Brianna's father."

"And what were you, Shane? What have you been all this time?"

"A friend," he answered simply. "Just a friend."

No, she thought. He meant more to her that than that. She loved him, wanted him to be a part of her life—her lover, husband, a stepfather to Brianna. She had wanted it all. The suddenly impossible dream.

What had become of the man who had made passionate love to her last night? Used her mouthwash this morning? Nibbled on her ear? Now all of it seemed like a lie, every last tender moment.

As she studied Shane's face, the determined line of his jaw and slant of his cheekbones, the truth became painfully clear. He could disregard her and Brianna so easily because they had only been a substitute for Tami and Evan, the woman and child he truly loved.

She reached for her daughter. "I have to go."

As she turned and walked toward her car, she kept her head held high. Shane stood behind her, but she didn't look back to see his expression. Pride was her companion, pride and a baby girl who had begun to cry.

Shane hadn't seen Kelly or Brianna for two days, and now they were leaving.

He paced the living room floor, checking his watch for the hundredth time. Kelly must be packing, preparing for her flight. Shane forced out a breath. Unable to stand the anxiety-ridden solitude a moment longer, he grabbed his keys from the coffee table and tore off out the door.

The drive to the cabin didn't take long, but by the time he arrived, his hands were clammy and his mouth dry. He parked beneath a tree and exited his truck. Her front door was open, just as it had been the first time he'd stopped by the cabin, the day she'd stood in the kitchen, eight-months pregnant, scrubbing the sink.

Shane approached the threshold, preparing to knock. As close as they had become, he realized he hadn't told her everything about himself. He hadn't admitted that he was afraid of spiders or that he...

His next thought grabbed his heart and squeezed it, leaving

a hollow ache. Loved her. He hadn't told her that he loved her.

He lifted his hand and rapped on the door, each knock pounding in time with his pulse.

"Just a minute!" she called out.

Silent, he waited, wondering why he had come. He couldn't ask her to stay. He wasn't the right man; he wasn't her baby's father.

Kelly walked toward the door and when she spotted him, she stopped, clearly startled. "I was expecting Tom."

"Sorry, it's just me." He didn't enter the cabin, and she didn't invite him in. "It's still a little early for my dad to come by, isn't it? He's still at work."

"I wasn't sure what his schedule was like."

Shane knew his father planned on being there to say goodbye. Tom was still welcome, even if his son wasn't. "I'm sure he'll be here before you leave."

"I'm still packing," she said, smoothing her dress in what seemed like a self-conscious gesture.

He liked the way she looked, her hair long and flyaway, her floral-print dress familiar. He wondered if she would still wear it once she got back to Ohio. It had a slight Western flair as it had come from the emporium in town.

How long would it take for the hurt to go away? he wondered. To be able to live in Texas and not think about her? Feel her presence in every flower that grew wild, every cloud that floated across the sky?

Shane looked down at his boots and noticed how scuffed they were. Jason probably wore nice clothes, designer fashions, sports coats and loafer-type shoes.

How could he have encouraged Kelly to marry her old lover? How could he have just given her to the other man?

Because of Brianna, he told himself. Because the baby was Jason's child, and that tied him to Kelly. It made them family. Shane had only been a pretend daddy to Brianna, a temporary lover to Kelly. He had no right to want them, to long to keep them.

"Is Sunshine awake?" he asked.

She nodded. "Yes."

"Would it be all right if I came in to see her?" He felt like a beggar in his scuffed boots and torn, ragged heart. A man on the edge of society looking in, a man who kept losing the women and children he loved.

Avoiding his gaze, Kelly stepped back and allowed him to enter. "Brianna's in the bedroom."

She led the way to the room Shane would never forget, the room that housed the bed where Brianna was born, the same bed Shane and Kelly had shared three nights before. He had known then that it was over, yet he hadn't been able to stop himself from touching her, from making love to her one last time.

The cabin would forever harbor ghosts, he thought. His, Puma's, Kelly's, Brianna's. And Butch's, too. Kelly's grandpa had spent his vacations there, an Ohio factory-worker who delighted in everything cowboy. What would Butch have thought about Shane and Kelly's love affair?

Maybe the old man knew. Maybe Kelly had talked to him about it in her prayers. Maybe she had told her grandpa that Shane Night Wind had chipped a piece of her heart.

He took a deep breath, defending his decision to let Kelly go. Her heart would mend, and her affection for him would fade. Jason had been her first love, the man she really wanted, the one she had cared about for years.

Taking another deep breath, Shane scanned his surroundings, then forced a smile. Brianna lay in her portable crib, kicking her feet, the toy cougar beside her.

He leaned over the padded rail. "Hey, little Sunshine."

The baby waved her arms, but he didn't pick her up. He couldn't bear asking for permission to hold Kelly's daughter.

"Your dad said he would ship the crib for me," she said as she folded clothes into a leather suitcase. "The swing, too."

"That's good." Shane noticed the tan-colored baby carrier he had bought for Kelly lay on the bed. He still had the blue

one. He had placed it in his dresser as a keepsake, he supposed. A sentimental item that would remind him of Brianna

Shane looked over at Kelly, and their eyes met in one of
those long, painful, awkward stares. He swallowed, and she
bit down on her bottom lip, both of them visibly shaken.

"I'm sorry," he said, his voice as parched as his throat. "I
never meant to hurt you."

"Don't...please," she responded, her eyes turning watery
her hands unsteady. "Don't try to explain it away. I don't
think I can handle it." She fidgeted with the suitcase, zipping
it shut. "I have to get Brianna ready."

"I'll go wait on the porch." He couldn't leave, yet he
couldn't stay inside with her, either. "I'll let you know when
my dad gets here."

Tom arrived an hour later, and soon the three adults gathered in the front room, Kelly holding her daughter. Shane lingered back, uncomfortable and uncertain of what to do. Would
Kelly let him hug her, kiss her one last time?

"I'm going to miss this little girl," Tom said as he reached
for Brianna.

Kelly's eyes misted. "She's going to miss you, too."

Brianna peered over Tom's shoulder at Shane, and he
smiled at the baby, the ache in his chest growing. Brianna
looked like a bright yellow flower, a golden-haired buttercup
dressed in summer ruffles, her tiny feet encased in shiny white
shoes.

"Thank you for everything," Kelly said to Tom, her eyes
clouding even more. "I don't know what I would have done
without you. You brought my daughter into the world."

"Promise you'll keep in touch. That you'll send pictures
and letters," the older man responded, his voice thick with
emotion.

"I will. I promise."

Tom kissed Brianna's cheek, then handed the baby to
Shane. While Kelly and his dad embraced, Shane held
Brianna, inhaling her powdery scent.

When the hug ended, no one spoke until Tom took charge

offering to load Kelly's luggage into her rental car. Within minutes Shane and Kelly were alone, Brianna still snug in his arms.

"Take care of yourself," he said, wishing he didn't have to let them go. He wanted to keep the mother and the child, pretend they belonged to him.

"You, too."

She took her daughter back and struggled to keep her tears from falling. Shane gazed into her watery eyes, knowing she wouldn't welcome his touch. A hug would only make her leaving that much harder.

"I better go." She turned away and headed out the door, her breath hitching as she lost the battle and began to cry.

Shane remained inside the rustic old cabin, whispering that he loved her, even though he knew she was too far away to hear.

Thirteen

Unable to face his father, Shane left the cabin alone and retreated to the rescue.

Looking up at the sky, he squinted. The sun rose high and bright—a yellow ball of warmth that left him cold and achy inside. Sunlight would forever remind him of Brianna, yet he knew nightfall would bring no solace. He would lie awake and think about Kelly, recall the taste of her lips, the feel of her touch.

Shutting out the world, Shane closed his eyes, avoiding the flowers that dared to bloom, their brilliance mocking his mood. God help him, he thought. He needed to see Puma, draw strength from the cougar's medicine.

Shane walked along the dirt path. With the volunteers gone for the day, and the animals resting in the shade, a hush lingered over the rescue. Even the air barely moved, the leaves on the trees still.

When he reached Puma's habitat, he stopped at the fence

nd called out in the cougar's language. He waited for a greet-
ng, and when he received none, he tried again.

Puma finally answered in a full-throated *"yaooow,"* and
hane responded in the same strong tone. The conversation
ontinued until Shane knew an invitation had been granted.
Ie entered the cougar's habitat and started toward the animal.
'uma lounged in his favorite spot, and when Shane neared,
he cat stood.

The magnificence of the mountain lion never ceased to
maze him. The danger and the beauty. He knew the drill.
Thrived on the thrill. *Never turn your back on a cougar. Use
ye contact cautiously. Read its body language. If it challenges
ou, look away. Don't roughhouse with a big cat; it can kill
ou in play.*

Shane leaned down and scratched Puma's chin, and the cou-
ar purred in response. The affection felt good, a temporary
alm.

"Maybe I could sleep here tonight," he said to the cat,
lthough he knew better than to invade Puma's territory. Too
uch time had passed since they'd lived together, and reliving
hose early days wasn't possible. Puma had grown and
hanged, and so had Shane.

The cougar lowered himself into a resting position, so Shane
ontinued to talk, knowing his friend was listening. "Kelly
ketched some incredible pictures of you, and we used them
n T-shirts and coffee cups. You're our mascot now. A sym-
olic figure for the rescue," he explained. "A good luck
harm."

Puma rumbled like a motorboat and rubbed his face against
hane's leg. He scratched the animal's chin again. "I'm glad
ou're pleased." He sighed and caught his breath. "I'm going
o miss her, Puma. So much."

The cougar nudged him and started to talk. A series of tiny
hirps. A message, Shane thought. A message he couldn't
omprehend.

"I wish I could understand you. But I can't. Not today."
nd maybe not ever. When Shane had let Kelly and Brianna

go, a part of him died—coiled and burned, then drifted int
dust.

He remained in Puma's habitat, touching the dirt, the leaves
the rocks that made up the animal's home. Nothing penetrate
him, nothing gave him strength. The land inside the fenc
wasn't his. It belonged to Puma, and as much as Shane like
to think they shared the same spirit, they were still two sep
arate entities. Mountain lions were loners. They didn't fall in
love, didn't mate for life. After a mating took place, a mal
assumed no further role. The female accepted full responsi
bility for the young.

Yet Shane, who thought of himself as part mountain lion
had fallen in love with Kelly, wanted to help raise her daugh
ter.

Suddenly Puma's message became disturbingly clear. Thi
time Shane couldn't rely on the cougar to mend his damage
heart. He would have to draw strength from his own medi
cine—the human soul that made him a man.

During the week that followed, Shane decided he didn't lik
being a man. He didn't like the loneliness, the ache that fol
lowed him each day. He wanted to go back to being a cougar
but Puma wouldn't let him. And Shane knew why. Hidin
inside himself would be cheating. He couldn't go on pretend
ing to be a loner when deep down he craved companionship
A family. The woman and child he had lost.

As Shane came through the front door, he could smell din
ner, a homey aroma of pork chops and mashed potatoes.

"Hi, Dad." He knew the food was supposed to enhance hi
appetite, make him feel better, but it only reminded him tha
two lonely men would be sharing the meal.

Tom turned away from the stove. "I have some news."

"Yeah?" Shane noticed the table hadn't been set. H
opened the top cabinet and removed two dishes. "What'
that?"

"Kelly called."

The dishes nearly slipped from his grasp. He had been wait

ng to hear about her, wondering, living in agony, barely surviving. "What did she say?" he asked, hoping he could handle
he blow—the news that Kelly and Jason had been working
hrough their differences. Sending her back to Jason had been
orture enough, but picturing them together made him ill. Kelly
with her butterfly wings and fairy-dust freckles and Jason with
a face Shane couldn't bring himself to conjure.

"She met with Jason," Tom said. "But it didn't go well.
Jason didn't even look at Brianna. He isn't the least bit interested in being that baby's father."

"What?" Shane's head reeled with sadness, confusion, a
rush of guilt-ridden relief. "I don't understand."

"Jason asked Kelly to lunch so he could present her with
a document outlining a financial settlement. He's willing to
pay for 'his mistake' as he put it, but that's as far as he'll
go." Tom leaned against the counter. "I got the impression
from Kelly that Jason was acting on the advice of some high-
profile attorney, offering a settlement so he didn't get slapped
with a paternity suit."

The sadness in Shane's chest grew deeper. An ache for
Brianna. Could the baby feel her father's rejection? "Kelly
doesn't want the money. She never did. All she ever wanted
was for Jason to care about his daughter."

When Shane's statement drifted too close to home, they
both fell silent. Tom pulled a hand through his hair, and Shane
studied his dad. Suddenly he saw reflections of himself, features he had never noticed before, little things—the arch of
their eyebrows, length of their fingers, shape of their nails.
Similarities that reminded him of the physical traits Brianna
must have inherited from Jason.

"Shane?"

Realizing he still clutched their dinner plates, he set them
on the table, his hands as unsteady as his heartbeat. "Yeah?"

"I know why you let Kelly go, why you encouraged her to
give Jason a chance."

"That doesn't matter—"

"Yes, it does," Tom interrupted, his voice edged with

shame. "It's because you didn't want Brianna to feel the pain
of being shut out of her father's life. You didn't want her to
suffer the way you had."

The tightness in his chest intensified. The ball of emotional
confusion. "This isn't your fault, Dad. I've forgiven you for
the past. We've both worked through that."

Tom's eyes turned a paler shade of blue. "But it still affects
your life. Your decisions." He paused and let out a breath,
the pork chops sizzling on the stove beside him. "Kelly loves
you, son. Loves you with everything she's got."

Shane's unsteady heartbeat quickened. "Did she say that?"

Tom shook his head. "No, but she didn't have to."

No, but she didn't have to. Hours later Shane sat on the
edge of his bed and picked up the phone, his father's words
echoing in his mind. Dialing the number the information op-
erator had given him, he waited for the other party to answer.

When a man came on the line, Shane squared his shoulders,
knowing his first encounter with Jason Collier had just begun.

Two days later Kelly sat across from her mother at their
dining-room table, toying with her breakfast. She appreciated
her mom's effort, the perfectly round stack of golden pancakes, but she didn't have much of an appetite. The single
daisy on the table was a thoughtful touch, too, but it only
reminded her of Shane and the wildflowers he'd picked in the
rain. She missed him desperately, and the reminder hurt.

"Eat up, sweetie, or you'll be late."

Kelly sighed. She had never been late for work a day in her
life. "All right." She cut into her pancakes and took a small
bite, wondering if the ache deep inside her would ever go
away.

Most people had weekends off, but Kelly worked them now.
Evenings, too. It was the only schedule that fit into her current
lifestyle. Neither she nor her mom could bear to have a
stranger watch Brianna, so Kelly worked the opposite hours
of her mother, leaving Linda free to baby-sit.

"I'm proud of you," Linda said. "You did the right thing with Jason."

She met her mother's gaze. "Thank you, that means a lot to me." Telling Jason to go to hell had been easy. She didn't want his "I'll-pay-for-my-mistake" money. She would provide for Brianna on her own. She would love and nourish her child. They wouldn't be rich, but they wouldn't be poor, either. Kelly would work extra hours to make holidays and birthdays special. And her mom would always be there, helping out. Like today. Fixing breakfast, baby-sitting Brianna and offering to drive Kelly to work since her own car was in the shop.

Linda lifted her tea. "I'm sorry he hurt you."

Kelly adjusted her napkin. "What I felt for Jason was just an infatuation. It's Brianna I'm worried about. She deserves better."

"Sweetie, I was talking about Shane."

Kelly caught her breath. How many years would pass before she stopped wondering where he was or what he was doing? "I'm okay, Mom. I'll survive." Because she had to. Because she had a baby to raise. A precious little girl with Kelly's fair skin, Jason's clear blue eyes and Shane Night Wind's heart-warming smile.

Shane entered the restaurant and took in his surroundings. He had never been to a country club before, but he thought the place was appealing in an austere, refined kind of way. He also knew that he didn't fit in, not with his rugged denim clothes and Western boots. But then he had agreed to meet Jason Collier on the other man's turf.

As the hostess led him to the back of the restaurant, he noticed several big picture windows overlooked acres of green. Golf. A sport Shane knew nothing about. He was definitely out of his element. A tall, broad-shouldered Comanche wearing plaid and putting after some little ball didn't quite cut it.

When the hostess directed him to his table, Shane came face-to-face with his opponent. Jason met his gaze, then stood and extended his hand. Proper, Shane thought. And wary. They were both wary.

He sat across from the other man and noticed the color of his eyes. Bright blue, like Brianna's.

"So you're from Texas," Jason said, his manners slipping as soon as the hostess was out of earshot. "The big, strong cowboy-type."

"Sorry," Shane corrected, the mockery setting him on edge. "I'm more the big, strong Indian-type. Comanche. We're a warring tribe."

Jason leaned back casually, but Shane knew he hadn't missed the warning. Suddenly, scalping the other man seemed like a damn good idea. Jason's light brown hair was styled with a bit too much mousse for Shane's tastes.

"Hmm." Jason studied his manicured hands, then looked up. "Now I'm not so sure you're on the level. Maybe Kelly sent you to kick my butt. Or up the ante."

"Kelly doesn't know I'm here. And your money has nothing to do with why I came."

The waitress interrupted with two tall glasses of water, a slice of lemon floating in each. Jason flashed a charming smile and ordered lunch, and when the waitress sent Jason an admiring look in return, Shane figured that practiced smile had fooled Kelly, too. She was too sweet, too trusting.

Shane declined to order, and the smitten waitress departed.

"Okay, so you're on the level," Jason said, resuming their conversation.

"That's right. I want to adopt your daughter. And marry Kelly, if she'll have me."

"Fine." Jason reached into his pocket, removed a business card and handed it to Shane. "That's my attorney's number. You can work out the details with him. He'll be more than glad to accommodate you."

Stunned, Shane stared at the card. That was it? "Don't you even want to know anything about me? Aren't you curious about what I do for a living? If I go to church? Pay my taxes?

Don't you care about what kind of husband or father I'll make?''

The other man raised an eyebrow. "Not particularly, no. If you want Kelly, you can have her. The kid, too.''

A muscle twitched in Shane's cheek. He could feel it ticking like a bomb. Telling himself to relax, he took a deep breath. ''Look, you're only twenty-four years old. Someday when you're older, you might wonder about your daughter. I'll understand if you want to keep in touch, if—''

''I'm twenty-five. And kids don't interest me.''

Cocky bastard, Shane thought, wishing he saw just a flicker of emotion in those icy blue eyes. Brianna deserved more. Much more. ''Then just listen, okay? I'll be the best parent I can be, but I won't lie to Brianna about who her biological father is. For the rest of your life, you need to remember that there's a little girl out there who carries your genes, and someday she might come looking for you.'' Leaning across the table, he drilled the other man with his gaze. ''And if she ever does, you sure as hell better be good to her.''

With that said, he pushed away his chair and stood. As he made his way to the door, the waitress passed him with Jason Collier's lunch. Shane nodded to the girl, then pocketed the attorney's card without looking back.

Tired and glad her workday was about to end, Kelly stood in the check stand, ringing groceries for a familiar customer. She knew most of the people who shopped at the market, and they, of course, knew her. Not personally, but enough to chat and smile. Unfortunately chatting and smiling took energy, and today hers was nearly sapped.

Glancing up to ask the last customer in line to pull the gate, an adrenaline rush hit her like a fist. Her knees threatened to give way, and the cereal box in her hand stumbled over the scanner, missing its mark.

A tall, dark-skinned man holding a blond, pink-cheeked baby waited at the end of the line.

Shane and Brianna.

She didn't have to look twice. He stood quietly, his shirt-sleeves shoved to his elbows, Brianna snug against his body, the side of her face peeking out of the cloth carrier.

He made eye contact, then smiled. Kelly wasn't sure if he had the right to smile at her, but her knees reacted again, buckling a little. Rather than meet that masculine smile, she pulled the cereal box across the scanner and reached for the last few items. Her current customer dug through an oversize purse and presented a small stack of coupons. She took them, hands shaking, heart bumping.

Why was he here? How could he rip her emotions to shreds, then walk into her place of employment a week later looking gorgeous and fit?

Kelly focused on her job. Drawing strength from the adrenaline pouring through her system, she made it through the next order, then found her voice and politely asked Shane to pull the gate. He latched it behind him, his gaze searching hers.

"I stopped by your house, and your mom told me you needed a ride home," he said when they stood face-to-face.

He flew in from Texas to drive her home? "My car's in the shop," she answered, unsure of what to do with her quaking hands.

Reacting to Kelly's voice, Brianna turned her head. Shane lifted the child from the carrier and held her up. "There's your mommy, Sunshine."

A smile brightened the baby's face, and Kelly's heart melted. She reached out to touch her daughter's cheek, and as she did, the proximity of Shane's body shifted the building, tilting her world. The one she had been living in without him.

"Why are you here?" she asked.

"To talk. Can we go someplace more private?"

He cradled Brianna, his hands gentle against the baby. They looked good together, she thought. The tall, powerful man and the bright-eyed little girl. Brianna seemed happy to be with him, content in his arms, blowing bubbles and gurgling.

"I can't leave just yet," Kelly answered finally. "I still have to run a tape on my till."

"Okay. We'll wait over there."

He nodded toward the gumball machines and smiled. A shyer smile this time, one that said he was a little unsure of himself, possibly nervous about their talk. His sudden vulnerability eased her quaking hands, and she began to cash-out her drawer on steadier ground.

Fifteen minutes later they headed out to Shane's rental car and strapped Brianna into the baby seat. Kelly sat beside Shane and faced the window, unsure of her emotions. Hurt, anger, anxiety, hope…she didn't know which one took precedence.

"I noticed a park on the way over," he said. "Can we go there? It's not as hot as it was earlier."

"That's fine." The muggy day had turned pleasant, the stifling heat dissolving into a soft breeze. "When did you get here?"

"This morning."

They drove in silence the rest of the way. An awkward kind of quiet, Kelly thought. When they reached the park, she expelled a sigh of relief. She needed air. Lots of it.

They claimed a shady spot beneath a tree. Shane removed a baby blanket from the diaper bag, spread it on a soft bed of grass and placed Brianna on it. She took to the outdoors immediately and closed her eyes, her tiny fingers curling.

Shane sat directly on the lawn and drew his knees up, his jeans a fluid line of blue against long, muscular legs. Kelly lowered herself to the ground, suddenly wishing she wore something prettier. Her work shirt wasn't the most flattering garment.

"I'm sorry," he said. "So sorry I hurt you."

Her emotions struggled to sort themselves out. She wanted to touch him, make sure he was real. "I can't believe you're here."

He released a heavy breath. "I saw Jason this afternoon."

Stunned, she sat staring at him. "What? Why?"

"To talk to him about Brianna. And you." Shane met her gaze, his eyes sending off sparks of gold. "I didn't like him,

Kelly. I wanted to kick his teeth in, but another side of me said 'This is the man who fathered Brianna and he deserves a chance to redeem himself.'"

The park and everything in it blurred. Tears, an oceanful, rushed her eyes. "And did he?"

"No." Shane shook his head and cast a gentle glance at the baby. "But I told him not to forget that he had a daughter, that she might seek him out someday." He fisted a handful of grass. "And if that happens, and Jason doesn't treat her right… I swear, I'll kill him."

The conviction in his voice had her catching her breath. "Did you tell him that, too?"

The corners of his lips tilted. "More or less. I figured he had it coming."

She wanted to kiss that smile—that warm, sexy mouth. "Thank you." He had come a long way to champion for a child. "You really are a friend."

He moved closer. "I hope I'm more than that."

Her heart pounded against her breast. "You said you weren't."

"I was wrong." He released the torn grass, and it fluttered back to the ground. "I'm the guy who loves you. Who wants to marry you and adopt your daughter."

A knot formed in Kelly's throat. The tears fogging her vision fell, and the woman inside her battled for control. No matter how long she had waited to hear those words, she couldn't accept his proposal. Not when she knew who Shane really wanted. She couldn't bear to be a substitute for Tami, nor could she allow Brianna to live in Evan's shadow.

"I don't think it's that simple," she said, hating the part of her that couldn't cheat, couldn't accept only half his love.

Shane glanced up at the tree, his pulse a quick, jittery ache. He could feel his heart teetering on a live wire. One push, one off balance step, one devastating answer and it would fall. Crash to the earth and die.

He brought his gaze to Kelly's, questioning hers. "You don't want me?"

She closed her eyes, then opened them, her fairy-dust freckles swimming in tears. He wanted to take her in his arms, hold what he had lost. But instead he looked over at Brianna, at her perfectly formed hands, the tiny body heaving with each sleeping breath. Her hair could have been a halo, he thought, a shimmer of golden light.

"I want you," Kelly said. "But I wish I didn't."

"Why?" He prayed he wouldn't lose his strength, wouldn't emasculate himself with tears a Comanche man wasn't supposed to cry. Kelly had a right to shed her emotions that way, but he didn't. "Please tell me why."

"Because I need to be your future, all of it, not just half."

Confused, he searched his mind to absorb her meaning. The sixth-sense he so often relied on had abandoned him. She talked in riddles, and his heart hurt. He wanted to marry her, love her for the rest of his days. Wasn't that the future? "I don't understand."

She rubbed at her face, pushing away tears. "I don't want to be a substitute for Tami."

"So that's it." Shane bit back a smile. He saw jealousy in her eyes, and God forgive him, he found pleasure in it. He had meant to clear the air about Tami, but Kelly's reaction to his proposal had jumbled his thoughts. "I called Tami before I came here. We talked for a long time. I told her about you and Brianna."

She gulped a breath, and Shane let himself smile. She looked like a teary-eyed waif. A sprite little butterfly. A beautiful urchin with wings. How could she doubt that he loved her?

"You talked to your ex-wife about me?"

"I had to. I needed the past to be over." And he needed to know that Evan was happy and well. "What Tami and I had was youth. There was no maturity in our love. It's different with you." He lifted her chin, refusing to lose her, to let her flutter those delicate wings and disappear. "What I feel for you is real. I'm not a boy anymore. I understand my heart."

And he wanted to give it to her, have her tuck it away for all time.

Kelly blinked. Happily stunned, he hoped. She leaned into him, a dizzy sort of glow on her face. "If you love me, why did you send me away?"

He inhaled the clean, summer fragrance she wore, the mist of watermelon that bathed her skin. "I sent you away because I thought I had no claim on your daughter. I thought I didn't deserve her because my blood doesn't run in her veins." He took Kelly's hands and held them. "And I was afraid Jason would lure you away, that your tie to him was stronger than what you felt for me."

"You were wrong. It's you I love." Her head found his shoulder, her body curling into his. "And now my daughter belongs to you, too."

Should he let himself cry? God only knew he wanted to. He stroked Kelly's hair and watched the baby sleep. His woman. His child. Magic and sunshine. "I kept battling with myself over Brianna. I wanted her to be mine. There were so many moments I forgot she wasn't."

Kelly pulled back to look at him, touch his cheek with a gentle hand. "You haven't mentioned Evan, Shane. Did you talk to Tami about visiting him?"

"No." There would always be a part of him that missed the little boy, but he knew Evan didn't need him. "Evan has a father. A good one from what Tami says. Too much time has passed. Me coming into his life would only confuse him. It wouldn't be fair."

"Maybe you could visit them as a family, see for yourself that Evan's happy. Maybe all of us could go. You, me and Brianna."

"Maybe." This woman, he thought, this delicate butterfly had spread her wings right before his eyes. He could see color all around her. Wildflowers and moonbeams. Beauty and love.

He brought his mouth to hers and felt a liquid response, her lips parting sensuously under his. Kelly Baxter was meant to be his wife. Of that, Shane Night Wind was certain.

* * *

Later that night Kelly reclined next to Shane on her bed. They were dressed for sleep, but both remained wide-awake.

"So this was your room when you were little?" he asked.

She nodded. "I've redecorated since then." But she knew it was still feminine. Grown-up frill, she supposed. The canopy over the bed draped a smooth beige fabric, the pillows down, their covers satin.

On a whitewashed dresser, she kept a collection of painted figurines. Mythical creatures—dragons and wizards, mermaids and unicorns. Shane seemed especially interested in the winged fairies. He had traced their tiny bodies with his finger, mumbling that he "should have known." Kelly didn't understand what he'd meant, but his fascination pleased her.

"We'll take this furniture with us," he said. "All of it. This can be our bedroom."

She tried to imagine her frill mixed with Shane's masculine decor—the dark rattan and solid oak cabinetry. It seemed right somehow—a blend of who they were.

She turned toward him, suddenly worried. "How can I leave my mom behind? She'll be so lonely here."

He shifted onto his side. "She can sell this place and come with us."

"And where exactly is she supposed to live?"

A mischievous grin tilted his lips. "With my dad."

Kelly bumped his shoulder and laughed. "Your dad and my mom. Granted, they're attracted to each other, but we can't expect them to live together right off the bat. They're too conservative for that."

"She can rent a room from him. That's proper enough. And he can find a job in her field. Maybe a bookkeeping position at this feline rescue I just happen to know."

She laughed again, delighted with the idea. "You've got this all figured out, don't you?"

"You bet I do. Our parents can keep the house, and we'll add on to the cabin. I can do the work myself. Besides, it's more us. An enchanted place with a rickety porch and flowers

peeking through the cracks. Smoke drifting from the chimney
sage and candles burning.''

The picture he painted made her think of her figurines—
fairies dancing in the moonlight, wizards conjuring potions, a
unicorn darting through a maze of trees. A magical cabin in
West Texas. Who would have guessed.

"I love you," she said.

"I love you, too." He kissed her then, a kiss vibrating with
need. A sudden gust of hunger.

She felt his muscles beneath her hands, the bunch, the flex
the unspoken language that had her lusting for more. She
roamed his chest, then caught the waistband of his shorts while
he lowered the straps on her nightgown and tasted a bare
shoulder.

She thought she heard music, Comanche drums mixed with
lilting harps and flutes—their music, their magic. Wizards and
warriors and tiny ladies with wings.

He was power, she thought, and passion—a man with fire
in his hair and copper melting over his skin. In his touch she
felt strength and beauty, a hard male body eager for hers.

Their clothes came away easily and drifted to the floor. She
slid her hand over his belly, then lower to stroke and caress
to watch his eyes shimmer, to listen to the sound of arousal
purr from his chest.

They kissed, over and over, absorbing the moment, the sen
sations only they could create. It was glorious to be naked
with him, to rub and tease, anticipate what erotic treasures
came next. A fluid hand, a moist tongue, a muscular leg tan
gled with hers. She felt everything—every subtle movement
every pore that opened, every nerve that jumped, every sigh
she breathed into his mouth.

He slipped into her without protection, arched his back and
rocked her body with slow, sexy strokes. She met his dizzy
rhythm, the feel of his flesh smooth and silky inside her own
They moved at a languid, dreamy pace—a gentle mating.

The music rushed back, filling her ears with splendor, he
mind with flowers and feathers, warbonnets and faraway

places only he could take her. He tongued her nipple and smiled. She held his head to her breast and watched him suckle, draw the peak into a moist, hungry mouth. Gripping his shoulders she raised her hips, desire swirling—its sensual voice calling her name. Teasing and begging.

"Tell me," he whispered. "Tell me what you want."

"You," was all she could say. "More of you."

He thrust deeper and gave her all that he was—his heart spilling love, his seed pouring warmth and promise into her womb. And at that moment, that incredible climactic moment when they were steeped in pleasure, liquid flames dancing between them, she knew they had become one.

Epilogue

At two-and-a-half, Brianna Night Wind chattered excessively, and smiled even more. Today she wore a pale lavender dress with puffy sleeves, ribbons, bows and heart-shaped buttons. A white lace petticoat peeked out from the hem, and ruffled socks flared at her ankles. Her shoes weren't scuffed—not yet, Shane thought, as she wiggled through his second attempt to straighten the barrette in her hair.

"Me bring Cougie to the church, Daddy."

"Of course you will." The barrette slipped again, and he grinned. Cougie was the toy cougar that had become her security blanket, the battered stuffed animal that followed her everywhere. She slept with Cougie at night, fed him breakfast in the morning, told him secrets and insisted he could purr. Brianna had her own form of mountain lion medicine, he thought. Her own brand of beauty and charm. She was, in his opinion, the most perfect child on earth—an angel with bright blue eyes and a generous heart. She prayed for everyone, people she knew and those she didn't.

"Where's Mommy?" she asked, shuffling her anxious feet.

"She's getting ready, too."

"Are you ready, Daddy?"

"Just about, " he answered, still struggling with the barrette
Brianna's soft curls rebelled.

Shane wore a black tuxedo and stiff white shirt, but his
jacket hung over a chair, and his feet were bare. Within the
hour Tom McKinley and Linda Baxter would be married in a
quaint little church just outside of town. Family members
would each have a special role in the ceremony, including
Shane's gypsy mother and her current lover.

"Mommy !" Brianna squealed as Kelly entered the nursery.
Shane lifted his gaze, his pulse suddenly tripping. A waterfall of flowers crowned her head in a spray of petals, and her
dress, a shimmer of lavender silk, draped luxuriously over a
swollen tummy. Kelly Night Wind was eight months pregnant,
and a more beautiful woman didn't exist. She glowed like
magic, a vision of maternal elegance.

He reached for Brianna and brought the child to her mother.
They huddled together as a family, in the circle of each other's
arms, secure and content.

Brianna patted Kelly's tummy and grinned. "Hello, baby,"
she said, happily greeting her unborn sibling.

As Shane and Kelly exchanged a proud smile, he searched
his wife's gaze. In her eyes he saw the world they had created—their private haven of happiness—the corner of Texas
where wildflowers bloomed and fairies fluttered their wings.
The place where exotic cats lolled in the shade, and men and
women fell hopelessly in love.

On this sunny afternoon they would celebrate a new marriage, the new life in Kelly's womb and a little girl who chased
away storms. For today, Shane knew, would lead the way to
forever.

* * * * *

You're not going to believe this offer!

In October and November 2000, buy any two Harlequin or Silhouette books and save $10.00 off future purchases, or buy any three and save $20.00 off future purchases!

Just fill out this form and attach 2 proofs of purchase (cash register receipts) from October and November 2000 books and Harlequin will send you a coupon booklet worth a total savings of $10.00 off future purchases of Harlequin and Silhouette books in 2001. Send us 3 proofs of purchase and we will send you a coupon booklet worth a total savings of $20.00 off future purchases.

Saving money has never been this easy.

I accept your offer! Please send me a coupon booklet:

Name: _____

Address: _____ City: _____

State/Prov.: _____ Zip/Postal Code: _____

Optional Survey!

In a typical month, how many Harlequin or Silhouette books would you buy <u>new</u> at retail stores?

☐ Less than 1   ☐ 1   ☐ 2   ☐ 3 to 4   ☐ 5+

Which of the following statements best describes how you <u>buy</u> Harlequin or Silhouette books? Choose one answer only that <u>best</u> describes you.

☐ I am a regular buyer and reader
☐ I am a regular reader but buy only occasionally
☐ I only buy and read for specific times of the year, e.g. vacations
☐ I subscribe through Reader Service but also buy at retail stores
☐ I mainly borrow and buy only occasionally
☐ I am an occasional buyer and reader

Which of the following statements best describes how you <u>choose</u> the Harlequin and Silhouette series books you buy <u>new</u> at retail stores? By "series," we mean books within a particular line, such as *Harlequin PRESENTS* or *Silhouette SPECIAL EDITION*. Choose one answer only that <u>best</u> describes you.

☐ I only buy books from my favorite series
☐ I generally buy books from my favorite series but also buy books from other series on occasion
☐ I buy some books from my favorite series but also buy from many other series regularly
☐ I buy all types of books depending on my mood and what I find interesting and have no favorite series

Please send this form, along with your cash register receipts as proofs of purchase, to:
In the U.S.: Harlequin Books, P.O. Box 9057, Buffalo, NY 14269
In Canada: Harlequin Books, P.O. Box 622, Fort Erie, Ontario L2A 5X3
(Allow 4-6 weeks for delivery) Offer expires December 31, 2000.

PHQ4002

Silhouette —

where love comes alive—online...

eHARLEQUIN.com

your romantic
books

- ♥ **Shop online!** Visit Shop eHarlequin and discover a wide selection of new releases and classic favorites at great discounted prices.

- ♥ Read our daily and weekly Internet exclusive serials, and participate in our interactive novel in the reading room.

- ♥ Ever dreamed of being a writer? Enter your chapter for a chance to become a featured author in our Writing Round Robin novel.

• • • • • •

your romantic
life

- ♥ Check out our feature article on dating, flirting and other important romance topics and get your daily love dose with tips on how to keep the romance alive every day.

• • • • • •

your
community

- ♥ Have a Heart-to-Heart with other members about the latest books and meet your favorite authors.

- ♥ Discuss your romantic dilemma in the Tales from the Heart message board.

your romantic
escapes

- ♥ Learn what the stars have in store for you with our daily Passionscopes and weekly Erotiscopes.

- ♥ Get the latest scoop on your favorite royals in Royal Romance.

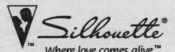